Tro

Zoe Chant

Shifting Sands Resort

This is the final book of the Shifting Sands Resort series. All of my books are standalones (No cliffhangers! Always a happy ending!) and can be read independently, but many of these characters reappear in subsequent books, and there is a series arc. This book in particular is chock full of spoilers for the rest of the series, so I suggest reading in order:

Chapter 1

There were several ways to get to Shifting Sands Resort that would have been faster than flying under his own power, but Mal enjoyed the journey and his dragon was grateful for a chance to spread his wings.

It was a long, leisurely flight, letting the world shrink beneath him to model scale. Whole countries were reduced to patchworks of farms and forests and wrinkles of mountains. The hours seemed short and Mal had a pang of regret as first the coast appeared beneath them and then the island that was their goal.

I am not winded, his dragon said wistfully. *I am strong and powerful. I could fly much longer than this.*

But the sun was beginning to set and Mal didn't want to be so rude as to try to check in after full dark.

The island was a brilliant green jewel on an ocean that was beginning to turn gold.

As beautiful as it was, Mal's sense of unease only increased as he approached.

The storms on the way were still distant, past the horizon; the only clouds were fluffy and harmless, stained in sunset colors.

But a swift, high circle of the island confirmed all of his worst fears.

There were weird currents of magic where there ought to be a smooth blanket of it and the tenor of the energy was off-key and unhealthy, like dark poison was running through veins in the earth. Something was very wrong here.

I almost waited too long, he realized in dismay. He'd been too tolerant of the resort owner's resistance to his plans, too interested to see what she would do next. His curiosity had almost been a disaster.

There was a particularly odd hiccup of power some distance from the resort, buried in the jungle, and Mal nearly went to investigate it despite the sinking sun. But his dragon gave a sudden burst of interest. *There*, he said urgently.

Mal folded his wings and dropped from the darkening sky to the sparkling resort below.

There! his dragon repeated, and they angled to land on the lawn downhill of a hall ringed in Greek columns near the top of the resort. Cheerful music and bright light streamed from the grand building.

Mal shifted so seamlessly he might as well have been descending a staircase, his luggage going from being cradled in claws to being carried effortlessly in human hands. He'd dressed in evening best, not wanting to meet the owner of the resort at any disadvantage, and he was glad now that he had; there was clearly a formal dance in progress.

The event hall was elegant and spacious. Couples were dancing and talking and drinking in a warm swirl of cheer and happiness.

Mal walked in slowly, picking out faces from among the many guests that were familiar from his investigations. The shyly laughing blonde would be Mary and the man she was dancing with was her mate and new husband, the former Marine, Neal.

There were two women browsing at the snack table; the towering amazon was Alice, and the brunette woman who would have been tiny even not standing next to her was Amber, her belly round with new life. Their mates, Grant—so recently still hiding under the name of Graham—and Tony respectively, were comparing notes by the bar where Tex, the cowboy bartender, was being distracted by a dark-skinned woman who was kissing his cheek. She had to be Laura and the woman who looked exactly like her was Jenny, the lawyer who had met him in battles of contracts many times... and hadn't always lost. Her mate, Travis, was tightening the connections on a chair nearby.

The reformed thug, Wrench, was dancing around the floor very staidly with flashy, dark-haired Lydia, the swan shifter in charge of the spa. Breck, the leopard shifter in waiter finery, was less restrained as he sashayed around with the strawberry-blonde Darla, spinning and dipping her. He wasted no opportunity to kiss her whenever the dance brought them together. Saina, a bindi sparkling at her brow, was dancing more serenely with Bastian, the lifeguard.

Then the dancers parted for a moment and Mal saw Scarlet.

The owner of the resort, the voice on the phone that brooked no nonsense and had a hundred ways of saying no. The mysterious woman who had reappeared after nearly forty years to restart the resort without a word of explanation.

Every one of his spies had agreed that she was unexpectedly powerful, and unexpectedly shrewd. They didn't have answers for his questions, only more puzzle pieces that didn't fit anywhere: she had great strength, keen intuition, and seemed to show up at the worst possible times.

A mercenary Mal had questioned extensively swore on his grandmother's grave that he'd shot the woman point-blank and hadn't harmed her at all.

And no one had ever seen her shift.

Alice, the last informant he'd sent in, claimed Scarlet had no shift form whatsoever and Mal had no reason to doubt her, even while it raised a whole garden of new questions. If she wasn't a shifter, what was she, and why would someone who *wasn't* a shifter invest so much energy into a resort that was exclusive to them?

She was certainly everything her photographs had promised... and somehow more. Her profile was elegant, and her up-swept hair was impossibly red in real life. The line of her neck was long and inviting and when she smiled at something, Mal had an unexpected moment of unsteadiness.

Curiosity made him put down his bags and make a swift, subtle gesture with a short murmur of words. Power swam into his vision by command and he was suddenly looking at the room with an overlay of *energy*.

Most humans had a spark of magic, just a hint, hardly worth noting. Normal animal shifters glowed with it; a slight aura all around them that reflected the strength of their animal, and the room was full of those. Saina, a siren, had a sparkling source of enchanted light around her human form and her dragon mate shone just as brightly. All of their mate bonds glimmered like curious flickers at the edge of his vision, connecting each of them no matter where in the room they were. It was unusual to have so many of them in one place, Mal mused.

Mal noticed Gizelle for the first time then. Her curious magic leaked from her in a fractured pattern where she sat next to her mate, Conall, as he played guitar with the band, her touch enabling him to hear. He was an extinct Irish elk and his glow was brighter than most normal shifters, if muted compared to the mythical creatures.

And they all might have been blown-out candles compared to Scarlet.

The light of her power swamped them all, even at this distance, behind the noise of all the dancers. She was intense, brilliant, streaming luminescence. Her energy completely blotted out the physical form beneath it.

So *much* energy.

She was *unimaginably* strong. Mal had never seen anything like it. The information he'd been given barely scratched the surface of what she was.

She had spotted him, he realized, blinking through the radiance. She put down her drink and began to weave her way gracefully through the dancers to greet him as he released the sight spell.

Even as normal sight returned, Mal could still sense the power shimmering from her. She was so potent that it sizzled all the air around her; people retreated from her path without recognizing it.

Of course she is that powerful, Mal's dragon said, his voice rich with desire. *A mate of ours would be no less.*

This complicated *everything*.

Chapter 2

Scarlet let herself enjoy the evening without reservation or regret.

The event hall was filled with light and laughter and music. Everything felt simply perfect.

The people she cared about most were all here, safe in the resort she had built to shelter them, and the future stretched out optimistically before her.

She had friends so close she considered them family, security at last... she even had a cat. Scarlet accidentally smiled fondly to think of Tyrant, and the middle-aged guest she was dancing with stumbled and went pale.

She tempered her smile and guided him back into the steps of the dance, careful not to draw him too close.

He was still glad when the music ended and Scarlet politely left him at the bar with a nod to Tex.

She mingled with the others, inquiring about their satisfaction with the accommodations, the food, the entertainment, and she was delighted by their genuine praise. Chef proved himself worth every penny, all over again, and Scarlet was pleased to coax stories of good service from several of the guests. She mentally filed stories to pass on in praise of the spa and the housekeeping.

She felt the new arrival just a moment before he arrived at the far door but took a moment to conclude her conversation with an elderly woman who was giggling with her about Breck's attentions during meals. "Such a *nice* young man," the woman said.

"He is," Scarlet agreed with a chuckle. Finding a mate hadn't stopped Breck from flirting outrageously, even if it meant less now than it ever had. "I'm sure he has saved a dance for you and I will send him over to collect on that in very short order," she promised. "If you will excuse me?"

The newcomer was tall and broad-shouldered, very appropriately dressed in a fine, tailored suit with just a touch of gold embroidery at the wrist. Dragon shifter, Scarlet remembered from the guest list, which made sense given the unscheduled arrival and the extravagant clothing. Mal Moore, her memory provided.

He was also, she thought wryly, rather stunningly good looking and it did unsettling things to her belly when he smiled confidently at her approach.

Down girl, she reminded herself. He was a guest. This was just a standard business meeting.

"Mr. Moore," she greeted with a hand extended politely. "Welcome to Shifting Sands Resort."

He stepped forward to take her hand and they ended up standing rather closer than she had intended. He didn't shake her hand, only held it in his strong fingers and looked down on her with an expression that might have been wonder in his warm brown eyes.

"Mal," he said. "You can call me Mal."

Scarlet tipped her head in acknowledgment. "Mal. My name is..."

"Scarlet. Scarlet Stanson."

The sound of her name from his mouth sent a shiver down her back and his hand, still holding hers, was terribly distracting. "Yes," she said, trying to regain her hand and her composure. She met handsome men all the time and managed to keep herself in control; she wasn't sure why this one should be any different.

"May I have this dance?"

In timing that was either terrible or utterly perfect, the band had just launched into a new song and Scarlet couldn't find—and didn't want to find—an excuse to say no. "Certainly," she said politely, and to her shock, he pulled her into a close dance position rather than open, one hand possessively at her waist, the other clasping hers.

She had to tip her chin up unexpectedly far to keep locked to his gaze and she was baffled that he didn't seem the slightest bit uncomfortable meeting her eyes.

For a few phrases of music, he led her effortlessly through the steps and Scarlet had to resist the urge to close her eyes and simply float blissfully in his strong arms. Her partners were usually more cautious with her, careful and afraid. He guided her out into a flashy spin and back in again.

Scarlet attempted to regain control of the situation when the music slowed. "Mal, is that short for Malcolm?" she asked conversationally, as if she didn't feel the slightest bit giddy.

He laughed, deep and intoxicating, and shook his head. "I should be so lucky," he said. He lowered his head as if he was imparting a great secret. "My given name is Normal."

Scarlet, suspecting a joke, chuckled. "Surely it isn't."

He sighed dramatically. "It is, I swear."

"Did your parents have such high aspirations for you?" Scarlet asked archly.

"They were forced into it. Dragon honor, you know."

He turned her, and for a moment Scarlet held her breath, wondering if he would dip her. He didn't, but there was a pause in the music where he simply held her and Scarlet felt like every nerve in her body was awake for the first time in decades and she was made entirely of all the longing she fought so hard to keep in check.

Then they were dancing a simple back and forth again and he continued. "When my mother was pregnant with me, she was crossing a busy street and tripped in front of an oncoming bus. She would surely have been hit and died if it weren't for a young man who pulled her out of the way. My father asked for his name, because in these cases, the least they were obligated to do was name me after him, but he refused, shrugging and saying that he was just a normal guy, doing the right thing."

"So they named you *Normal*?" Scarlet really did laugh then, and Mal grinned at her in a way that made her tingle to her toes.

She dampened her merriment with determination, but could not quite keep from smiling back at him. "Most people would go with their middle name in such cases," Scarlet observed.

"I assure you, my middle name is even worse," Mal said with a suffering sigh. There was something familiar about his voice...

The music was swelling again and he led her into a turn away from him so that Scarlet was looking away when everything crashed into place and she finally realized who this had to be.

Normal. *Normal* Moore, with an unlikely middle name and a common last name. N. Moore. N. *Padrikanth* Moore, Beehag's vindictive lawyer: the man who had been attempting to roust her from the island for more than a year, trying to woo away her staff and destroy her business.

Scarlet slipped from his grip and had to temper her desire to turn and punch him in the middle of the dance floor. She had stalked halfway across the hall to the far exit when he caught her—or tried to.

"Scarlet," he called. "Wait!" He seemed puzzled when he couldn't catch her arm. She wasn't about to let him touch her again.

She turned and met his eyes with blazing fury.

"Get out," she said quietly between gritted teeth. "Get out of my resort and off my island." It was a growl, and no part of the threat was *veiled*.

He should have backed off. Anyone else would have left his bags and *fled* in the face of her anger.

But Mal, *N. Padrikanth Moore*, only stepped *forward*. "I have a reservation," he said, maddeningly.

And dammit, he did. *Mal* Moore was a registered guest, with a signed contract, and Scarlet was forced to honor that.

"You are a guest," she conceded, furious. "Cottage four. It's unlocked, I'll have a key delivered to you in the morning. If you have *business* with me, you can make an appointment and I will see you with my lawyer. You have her number."

"I need to speak with you about the offer you made," Mal said swiftly.

"You can't stop me," Scarlet snarled and this time she was the one who stepped forward, every inch of her bristling in challenge. "You can try your dirty tricks and your pretty promises on someone else, but you will *never* take this place from me."

The hall was silent. Scarlet wasn't sure if the song had ended or if the musicians had simply stopped playing, but she was suddenly aware that all of the guests and all of the staff were watching from the other end of the hall.

"Scarlet," he said, too quietly for them to hear, "please stop being so *stubborn*."

That was the voice she knew from dozens of staticky phone calls: that infuriatingly superior attitude, that pretense of being reasonable.

"You are a *guest*," Scarlet repeated through clenched teeth. "Please enjoy the amenities we have to offer and contact a member of the staff if you have any problems or questions."

Then she was stalking away, through the door, and gone.

Chapter 3

Mal did not sleep well, despite the luxurious bed and its billion thread-count Egyptian cotton sheets, and he lay in them long after the sun rose, trying to make sense of everything.

His thoughts kept returning to the betrayal and anger that had bloomed in Scarlet's face when she realized who he was, and the soft, yearning laughter that fiery look had replaced.

She was so beautiful, so powerful. Those green eyes, that glossy hair that no photograph did justice to... He longed to see if she tasted as potent as she felt, to bury his fingers in her hair, to lay her down and claim her.

She is ours, his dragon rumbled, but Mal remembered the fury in her face and knew that it was more complicated than that.

Mal was not used to second-guessing his methods or questioning his own decisions, but he found himself thinking over every interaction they'd ever had. Had he done her as wrong as she was clearly convinced he had?

He rolled out of the bed and stalked to the desk where he'd left a folder open the night before.

The top photo was a candid, close-up shot of a beautiful woman with candy-red hair wearing a crown of deep green holly.

Scarlet Stanson.

His mate.

She was smiling in this photo, as she was not in so many of her others.

Mal frowned thoughtfully in return.

He understood people, especially shifters. He knew how they worked and what made them tick. After more decades than he cared to admit as a lawyer, he could predict what they would do under pressure with eerie accuracy, and he used that knowledge to his advantage.

But he didn't understand Scarlet Stanson.

He shuffled back to an older photograph, faded with age. It was another Christmas shot; a pine tree in the background was draped in old fashioned lights and tinsel. Scarlet's hair, nut brown, was swept up in exactly the same bun and she looked like someone had surprised her.

Last night hadn't been the first time she'd surprised *him*.

She had failed at every turn to fall into the patterns he had expected of her, bucked his expectations and thwarted his plans.

And she wasn't just a small problem.

The island was never meant to have been developed. Alistair Beehag's private compound was bad enough, but a resort? And not just a quiet, garden variety resort. Beehag's partner, Lord Aaric Lyons, had built a luxury resort designed just for shifters.

Mal had been glad when Lyons vanished and the resort stalled out before he had to interfere. He spent a few years working his way into the Beehag family as their lawyer and was as alarmed as they were when Scarlet Stanson mysteriously reappeared. She had brilliant red hair but didn't look a day old-er and she pointed out the language in a binding contract for lease that even he could not find loopholes in. Within a year, she had the resort opened for business.

Still, he thought he had time. Decades even, and Mal had always excelled at the long game.

So he waited for her to fail on her own and was surprised when she didn't. She collected a fascinating array of skilled staff, finished the half-built resort in remarkable time, and courted in a chef who could have cooked in the finest restaurants anywhere in the world.

When Alistair Beehag's atrocious shifter collection—a terrible zoo where shifters were forced to remain in their animal form—had been uncovered and the prisoners released, Mal had been furious and had nearly taken the opportunity to rid himself of *all* the problems on the island at once.

But Scarlet unexpectedly took in all the refugees from Beehag's menagerie, before Mal could step in. Mal had been so shocked by the act that he put the rest of his plans on hold, sparing the resort until he saw how the chips fell out.

It was a stunningly poor business move. The resort had barely begun to establish itself, and yet she'd chosen to run her finances—Mal had access to all of them—dangerously into the red in an act of pointless charity. She tied up dozens of rooms that could otherwise have been booked for people who would never be in a position to repay her and hemorrhaged thousands of dollars a day to feed them, clothe them, and send them back to their old lives when they were ready.

None of them were important people, none of them had connections that would serve her. She'd done it, as far as Mal could tell, completely selflessly. She was too smart not to realize how thin she'd stretched herself, even if she appeared to keep the true depths of her debts—already considerable—secret from the staff.

And she didn't give up.

Instead, she hooked a contract for a male shifter beauty pageant, with impressive and flattering media coverage, and business boomed. She even managed to host one of the highest profile shifter weddings in decades.

Mal picked up the newest edition of *Night Shift*, a glossy shifter gossip magazine and had to smile wryly at the splashy cover. A giant cave bear and a leopard were facing off and a distraught bride in the background wearing pounds of jewelry was wringing her hands. Guests were fleeing and potted plants were toppling.

Scarlet didn't feature much in the photos; she was a blurry, bright-haired figure in the background at most, but Mal had gotten several first-hand accounts of the tawdry event. The wedding had dissolved into chaos, the bride had run away with a waiter, and Scarlet had shared choice words with the mother of the bride publicly, quoted in damning detail within the article. The lawsuit that had been filed against the resort was a veritable tome of complaint; a copy of it sat on his desk next to the folder.

Mal almost felt guilty for his part in the pandemonium.

Almost.

The waiter, Breck, still worked at the resort with his runaway bride. As did the washed up mermaid, Saina, the twin sisters Jenny and Laura (who had fled here from the mob), and

Wrench, the brute with the unsavory past who had tried to kidnap the wrong one of them for money.

Scarlet had shown them all utterly illogical compassion and they had returned her trust with loyalty that gave Mal considerable pause; they had denied every tempting offer he had dangled in front of them and ignored every subtle attempt to sow discord.

All because of Scarlet.

And Scarlet herself was a cypher. How had she managed to win such devotion from her staff? She had even convinced Grant Lyons to shake off his identity as Graham Long and claim his first right of refusal to buy the island itself. The staff had scrounged the exorbitant price of the sale in nickels and dimes and gifted it to her in entirety.

Mal trailed his hand across the offer that they'd sent, shaking his head in grudging admiration, and then began to get dressed. Mal had managed to keep a life insurance policy owed to Laura and Jenny tied up in paperwork for almost a year and he'd scared two buyers off from buying Conall's business—Conall was a permanent resident retiring from a life of celebrity as a classic musician who had built a business empire and given it all up to settle down on the island with his skittish mate Gizelle, one of the longest imprisoned and most damaged residents of Beehag's cruel menagerie.

But Mal hadn't counted on Magnolia, another of the resort's permanent residents, reconciling with her royal family and regaining access to her inheritance, or on a third buyer for Conall's music empire appearing out of the woodwork while he was still busy with the second.

He had no legal recourse to stop the sale.

It was downright sloppy of him to let them get this far, build this much hope.

Then there was the fact that Scarlet was, completely beyond expectation, his *mate*.

She was so beautiful, so strong, so... vulnerable.

And she was going to be *crushed* when the resort inevitably fell.

A knock at the door interrupted the unavoidable spiral of his thoughts.

He opened the door to find a curvy, dark-skinned woman holding out a key and a brochure.

"Ms. Smith," he greeted.

She smirked at him. "That's a safe guess," she said mockingly. "But it's my sister you'll be needing to see if you have any business to discuss."

This was Laura then, the wolf shifter who had married the cowboy bartender, identical twin to the lawyer Jenny. "Thank you," Mal said gravely, accepting the items. The resort hadn't upgraded to keycards; it was an actual key on a large wooden keychain.

"Breakfast is open for another few hours," Laura added. "Scarlet said you are to be treated exactly like any other guest and that you are... *welcome*... to enjoy the amenities."

Her emphasis suggested that *welcome* was not exactly what he could expect, but Mal only said, "I appreciate it."

Once she left, he was dismayed to find that he was hungry. It had been a long flight the night before and his dragon's appetite was considerable... even if food was his second choice.

The restaurant was not terribly busy, but several of the tables were in use when Mal arrived. He seated himself at the edge of the deck, overlooking the bar and the pool beyond.

The waiter, sharply dressed, plunked a glass of ice water down in front of him and gave him a distinctly unfriendly appraisal. "Chef is making custom omelets this morning. We have most ingredients you could want in stock to build your own, or you can choose from a Denver—a proper Denver, with no cheese—or a vegetable lovers that uses what's fresh with mozzarella. Do you need a moment to decide?"

He waltzed to the next table without waiting for Mal's answer and spent notably longer chatting up the guests and flirting with the matron of the group.

Breck. Mal remembered vividly his role in the recent wedding disaster and he was amused to note the dragon runes that circled one of Breck's wrists when he reached to refill a water glass. Mal fingered the long sleeves of his own light bamboo shirt thoughtfully.

The waiter took the order for the second table back to the kitchen, served a third table, refilled drinks throughout the restaurant, and finally returned to Mal's table, his slight obvious. "Have you decided?" He did not offer to refill the half-empty water glass, despite the towel-wrapped pitcher he held.

"Vegetable with a side of bacon," Mal said serenely. "Coffee."

"There's bacon at the buffet," Breck said dismissively, and he turned coldly away.

Mal did not expect his meal to come without a generous seasoning of spit and briefly considered feeding himself solely from the buffet. It was clear that the staff knew exactly who he was and had no qualms making sure that he knew exactly how little they cared for his presence.

It wasn't entirely unexpected.

He'd already tested their loyalty to Scarlet and found it impenetrable. It must look, from their narrow view, as if he had some kind of vendetta against her, or against the resort itself.

The omelet came cold and late, neither of which could quite disguise the quality of it. The vegetables were stunningly fresh and perfectly cooked and the white cheese was a good pair with the fluffy eggs. It was served, despite Breck's earlier brush-off, with a generous platter of thick, salty bacon, and a stout cup of strong, good quality coffee (also nearly cold).

Mal ate it without complaint and did not bring attention to his empty water glass, despite Breck's several circuits of the room with the pitcher.

He left his starched napkin on the table when he had finished and went to the railing that overlooked the bar and the glimmering pool below that. It was a tasteful paradise, with shining tile, perfectly groomed foliage, and grand, Greek-style columns.

It was really no wonder Scarlet didn't want to let go of it.

Mal leaned onto the railing, then shifted as he kicked off, launching from the deck on mottled golden dragon wings. Sunbathers around the sapphire pool looked up in wonder as his dragon form passed over, gleaming in the sun.

Showing off a bit? Mal asked. Mythical creatures were usually invisible to humans and regular shifters, but they could choose to be seen.

She should see and admire us, his dragon said smugly as they circled over the resort. *The light here is flattering.*

We have work to do, Mal reminded him. *Let's focus.*

Chapter 4

Scarlet stalked into the early afternoon senior staff meeting and glared them to silence.

They stared back, clearly dying of curiosity over the events of the night before but not quite willing to ask.

"The resort will be at just over sixty percent capacity this week," she said coolly. "We've got a request in for a whale spotting tour later this afternoon—Travis, can I put you down for that?"

Travis agreed. "Not a problem. The solar panel on cottage seven just needs to be wired in, and that's the last one."

Scarlet nodded. It had been an expensive investment and the panels were only installed at a few cottages so far, but if they could start moving away from pricey fuels that had to be imported from the mainland, it would be worth it. If she could just keep her resort long enough to see the payoff... she caught her hands curling into fists as she thought about Mal... *N. Padrikanth Moore.*

"We have two guests of particular note coming in on the morning charter," Scarlet said, consulting her notes with a scowl. "One is an elderly domestic cat shifter who has mobility issues. I've talked with her companion and will be putting her at cottage twenty-two. Liam, that's right there next to your elders, because we've got the most access infrastructure in that area and it won't involve stairs to reach the restaurant."

Liam, who was in charge of a small shifter retirement community within the resort, nodded agreeably. "I'll reach out and see if she's interested in some of the activities we've got scheduled. She can take meals with our crew, if that's convenient."

Scarlet nodded crisply. "Thank you. The other guest requiring special consideration is a fire ant shifter. I want any pest control to be extremely careful this week. I would like to maintain our good record of not having squashed any guests."

There was a cautious wave of chuckles through the room, and then expectant silence.

Scarlet, knowing what they were really dying to ask, nodded instead at the large, gray-haired man sitting at the side of the room in an apron. "Chef, if you'd like to start off our department reports."

She remained standing as he confirmed the status of inventory. He added, "I'd like to have Travis look at the grill; I feel like it's acting a little sluggish, not running quite as hot as usual. Oh! And I'm down fifty pounds of salt. I'll need to have some picked up from the mainland before the end of the week."

Scarlet furrowed her brow at him. "Fifty *pounds*?" Chef was usually excellent at inventory management and this was a significant quantity.

"An unopened bag went missing from storage yesterday. I've looked every place it might have accidentally been put, but it's just gone."

"Stolen?" Wrench asked swiftly. Scarlet had placed the tattooed panther shifter in charge of security and he was taking his new duties very seriously. There was almost no crime at the resort, and she rarely needed additional enforcement, but she suspected that it would give the guests peace of mind to know that there was someone in charge of such matters. Most of all, it made Wrench feel like he had a purpose; he refused to take his mosaic art seriously, though Scarlet was encouraging him to continue his work.

"Who would steal salt?" Travis asked, laughing. "The whole bag costs less than ten dollars, and there's not much black market use for it."

"Someone with a vendetta against snails?" Breck suggested.

Others chuckled, Scarlet made a note to order the salt, and the meeting passed to Breck, who gave an entertaining report about the service schedules, and then to Graham.

"If you're going to borrow my tools, you'd better put them back," the lion shifter growled. "I'm missing a shovel from the uphill storage room. Putting in two new beds of herbs, have a surplus of lettuce, the lower paths need raking, I'll get on that tomorrow before it's too hot."

"Salt and now a shovel! It's an out-of-control crime spree!" Breck observed drolly. "Wrench, you'd better get on this!"

Wrench gave a grunt that might have been a laugh.

"No one would steal from Grant Lyons, King of the Jungle," Travis joked. "A shovel made of pure gold wouldn't be worth that risk."

A swift smile crossed Graham's face at the sound of his previous name and fighting title; he had somehow found a sense of humor when he'd met his mate, Alice, and Scarlet caught a smile of her own briefly on her face.

Smiling managed to remind her of Mal, of his self-assured grin and the feeling of his hand at her waist.

"Lydia," she said, more sharply than she meant to. "Anything we should be aware of at the spa?"

She only caught about half of Lydia's report, stewing over the sheer gall of Mal Moore, showing up here, at her resort, under the guise of being a guest. What did he think he could accomplish in person that he couldn't over dozens of phone calls and letters? In what world did he think that he could convince her not to go forward with the offer for the resort? He must be desperate, knowing that he had no legal recourse to stop her.

Or maybe he thought that his charms could persuade her in person where they'd failed over distance?

Scarlet didn't realize how angry she had gotten until she snapped the pen she was holding and everyone went silent and stared at her.

"Thank you, Lydia," she said as mildly as she could manage. "Tex?"

Tex drawled a bar report, requesting some mixers and reporting a broken tap for Travis to look into.

"Is there any other business?" Scarlet finally asked, finishing her notes with half a pen.

There was a brief moment of anticipatory silence, then Breck asked boldly, "I don't know... *is* there any other business?"

Scarlet glowered at him. "I think we're done here," she said dismissively.

She left the room swiftly and heard the conversation lift into gossip and speculation behind her.

"THANK YOU FOR PLAYING last night," Scarlet said to Conall sincerely, gravely accepting his offer of a glass of water. "Performing has never been a part of your contract and I don't want to take advantage of your kindness."

Conall poured them each a glass of water from the icy pitcher at the small kitchenette. "I don't feel taken advantage of," he assured Scarlet as he turned back and gave her the glass. "It's a pleasure to be able to play again." He gave the young woman in the living room a quick, amused smile, but she didn't notice.

Gizelle was lying on her belly on the couch, engrossed in something on her tablet. Her bare legs were up in the air behind her, ankles crossed, and there were headphones over her ears. The cord, Scarlet noticed, had been chewed on, probably by Gizelle's kitten, Sweet One. The young gray cat was on the back of the sofa just above Gizelle, curled up asleep.

Scarlet smiled as they sat across from each other at the dining room table. "They were extremely excited to have played with you." Conall, as a young musician, had been on a skyrocket to success. He produced several bestselling albums and garnered several awards before a car accident stole his hearing.

He had come to Shifting Sands a bitter, angry man, resentful of his loss and disenchanted with the fast-paced, highly successful business life he had tried to use to replace music.

Gizelle had changed everything for him.

Shy and frightened, his mate had lived all of her life imprisoned by a madman, trapped in her gazelle form. She had no memory of the time before her rescue and few social skills. Neal Byrne, one of her fellow prisoners who had been key in releasing the inmates of the zoo, had helped coax her back to human shape, but it was Conall's love that had made her truly bloom.

Her greatest gift to him in return was arguably the ability to hear again; when she touched him, particularly skin to skin, he could hear again, using her ears.

But Scarlet was fairly sure that his ability to smile again was actually the most precious thing that Gizelle had given him.

He was smiling now and he put his hand across the table to take the paperwork that Scarlet had put down. He had to scoot the papers around a curious centerpiece: a heavy lump of unattractive metal that had once been a lock on one of the cages of the zoo where Gizelle had been imprisoned. It had been a gift from her, the most precious item of her possession. Conall sometimes carried it with him, despite its awkwardness, and it had been fitted with a carabiner to hang off his belt.

"These are the revisions to the lease, provisional to the purchase of the island." Scarlet let herself feel a moment of grateful wonder and anticipation. The idea that she would own the island and never have to worry about it being taken from her again was still fresh and new.

"Beehag hasn't accepted the offer yet?" Conall said, glancing through the paperwork.

"He has thirty days to accept per the contract," Scarlet said as serenely as she could manage, remembering the feeling of Mal's hand at her waist as they danced instead of how he had tried to weasel the resort away from her. "Jenny says there's no reason they shouldn't simply accept, but I suspect Beehag's lawyer will wait the full window just to be a jerk about it." An unexpectedly *hot* jerk, it turned out.

"How is she?" Scarlet asked, lowering her voice. She didn't have to worry about Conall hearing her; without Gizelle's touch he couldn't hear her at all and was relying on his ability to read her lips.

"She's nervous about something," Conall said honestly in return.

"Neal...?" Gizelle had been anxious about Neal's return to the resort to marry his mate Mary; she had changed so much since he had left and come so far from the gazelle who wouldn't shift to human.

Conall shook his head firmly. "She talked with him before their wedding and as far as I can tell, that's all fine now. No, this is..." he shrugged, looking over at the couch where Gizelle's bare feet suggested she couldn't hear anything outside of her earphones. "It's getting hard to hear," he said thoughtfully. "The background noises she hears are getting worse. It's like being surrounded by a hundred radios playing different stations that are mostly tuned to static, and they've all gone up a notch lately."

"The voices of more shifter animals," Scarlet suggested. It had been a surprise to the staff when Conall revealed that Gizelle could hear their animals. Conall had been quick to explain that it wasn't anything that could be considered eavesdropping—only when she touched a shifter did their animal's voice come into focus.

"Sometimes I think it's more than that," he said reluctantly. "It's been getting... louder? Clearer? There are more voices, even though there are no more guests? It's hard to pinpoint. And..." Conall looked uncomfortable. "She's been talking about the end."

"Death?" Scarlet glanced at Gizelle's feet, her fragile toes flexing. "It's a concept she may only be starting to understand. There are so many things that she's never faced before." She had a pang of empathy. "It's a big world and there's so much I wish she could be sheltered from."

Conall frowned at her mouth and Scarlet wondered if she would need to repeat herself until Conall shook his head. "She doesn't seem to be fixated on death, she seems very matter-of-fact that the end—her end—is coming, and she talks about things that are her fault, and how she's got to figure out how to fix things. Her fugue states are happening more often lately, like they're getting harder for her to ignore."

Scarlet frowned in sympathy. "There's so much we don't understand about her." She finished her water. "Is there anything I can do to help?"

Conall shook his head and stood to gather their glasses. "I will read over the revisions and let you know if I have any changes after I've conferred with my lawyer," he promised.

Theirs was an efficient friendship, Scarlet thought with amusement as she stood. They didn't tend to waste words, but their mutual affection for Gizelle gave them a broad common ground that they had built a sturdy companionship upon. She was grateful for that friendship, even as it left her craving for something deeper.

Her thoughts returned without bidding to Mal—Mr. Moore.

She stood, dismissing her thoughts fiercely. Mal Moore was a thorn in her side, a problem to be dealt with, not danced with. "Thank you. Let me know if you have any concerns."

As she walked past the couch, Gizelle suddenly slipped off her headphones and fixed her with a wide-eyed look as she righted herself. "Do you know about sonic booms?" There was a physics lesson paused on her tablet.

"A little," Scarlet said. Physics had never been a topic of particular interest, but she had slogged through a few years of study. "It was a long time ago."

Gizelle was happy to explain, bouncing to her feet. "All the sounds want to go fast but they can only go one speed, the speed of sound, and they get all backed up in one wave that hits you at once and it's like a great big explosion."

"It really is fascinating," Scarlet agreed. Gizelle's enthusiasm was contagious.

"Can people make sonic booms? They're all trying to go so fast, but can only go the one speed through time. Will they get all backed up and explode, too?"

Scarlet looked at Conall helplessly, but Gizelle was speaking obliquely and he couldn't read her lips.

"I have no idea," Scarlet said. "But it certainly paints a vivid picture."

"No," Gizelle said thoughtfully. "Not a picture, a song." Then she scolded, "Oh, Sweet One, no!" because the kitten, startled out of sleep, had slipped down onto the couch and was extending a paw at the headphone cable. "Conall has already bought me three of those!"

Scarlet chuckled as she slipped out of the door; she had already gone through at least a half dozen of her own various cables thanks to Sweet One's sister, Tyrant. It had amused everyone when the cream-colored cat had attached herself to Scarlet instead of Gizelle, and Scarlet was grateful for the companionship, even while she sometimes found herself frustrated by the creature's destructiveness.

Outside of Conall and Gizelle's cottage, Scarlet turned her feet to the central path running up the resort and she allowed herself a moment of pride looking up over the resort. White columns and glossy tiles graced the gorgeous central buildings of the resort and everywhere, verdant green trees and flowering bushes cast cooling shadows and provided pockets of privacy.

She'd done well, she thought.

The resort was finally thriving, and—her heart squeezed—it was finally almost *hers*, outright. It was a safe place, the haven for shifters that she'd always imagined it could be. It was just the right touch of luxury and practicality, beauty and durability.

Mal's presence here... surely that was just some final bluster before the sale was finalized. He couldn't stop her, he didn't have any legal leg left. And if he was hoping to come win her with his admittedly considerable masculine charms, he was about to find out exactly how practiced she was in ignoring the desires of her body.

Chapter 5

Mal pivoted on a wingtip and flew over the crescent of golden sand beach, then followed the edge of the sea on the west coast of the island.

He extended his senses, the runes etched into his scales momentarily flaring with light.

The flow of power was as bad as he'd feared coming in the night before. It was like looking at a bad light ballast in a dark room, dim and flickering. The spell he had come to renew—a spell that should be steady for decades more—was *failing*.

Another little white beach opened up, a tiny half-circle bisected by a river that snaked from a beautiful waterfall. Cliffs on all sides isolated it. Under other circumstances, Mal might have been tempted to stop and bask in the warm sunlight.

But worry drew him on, the island rising to his right, the ocean stretching to his left, as he flew north. The dock for Beehag's compound appeared and Mal swung inland and rose into the air with powerful wingbeats, following the steep, winding road.

The compound was half-destroyed; the Phoenix had done his work well, and the zoo had been scorched to the earth in many places; no full cages remained. The arboretum was crumbling. The lawns that had been so tidy and well-groomed when Mal had last been here, many years ago, were overgrown.

There was a beaten-down area in the center of the zoo, the grass trampled to brown.

Mal circled it curiously, then reconciled it with the Civil Guard report he'd intercepted the week before; this would be where the fighting ring had operated, pitting Grant Lyons in a handicapped revenge match.

With wingbeats that raised dust, Mal found the sturdiest of the remaining walls and perched.

He shifted back to human.

From his vantage point, he could see the encroaching rainforest. The rain must not be as frequent here; it seemed less vividly green than the jungle that ringed the resort.

He gave a casual murmur and gestured. Energy overlaid his sight once again.

This was a passive spell; he didn't wish to further muddy the evidence, or cause more damage inadvertently. He paced to one end of the wall and stared down at the burned zoo. Traces of the Phoenix's magic teased at the edges of his vision, and Corbin's contaminated power was like a distasteful oily smear over the entire area, rainbow hued with the flavors of the mythic shifters he and his followers had been draining.

Corbin, Mal thought in disgust. Corbin could be the cause of this disruption. With his ham-handed, stolen magic, he might have disturbed the carefully laid spell.

Mal could tell, just from the evidence left, that Corbin had been loud, unconstrained, unrefined. But it didn't feel... focused. He'd been a child with a canon, so self-absorbed and noisy that he probably hadn't even *realized* there was anything beneath the island.

Beneath him, the ground suddenly rumbled, and the trees shuddered. The wall he was on even swayed for a moment. Then, as quickly as it had come, the earthquake was over, leaving Mal coursing with adrenaline.

He centered himself, once the earth stopped moving and he was sure the danger had passed.

Curious, his dragon said as an understatement. His voice had a current of worry, which was itself worrisome. Mal's dragon was a well of confidence and apprehension rarely intruded from that quarter.

Mal gathered himself and shifted as he leaped from the wall, a strong downbeat of his wings bringing him into the air over the compound.

He flew back to the resort following the east coast, over the primitive airstrip, along the winding road to the resort.

After the abandoned and destroyed Beehag property, the resort was like a gleaming jewel, beautiful and perfect. But Mal's dragon, for once, was not interested in beauty; he was focused on the low building at the top of the resort with the open courtyard.

Our mate, he insisted. *We have to get her away from here.*

With effort, Mal kept him from landing at Scarlet's office and trying to force her into fleeing with them. *We have some time*, he reminded his dragon. And he already knew that trying to force Scarlet to do anything was a losing game.

Not much time, his dragon countered unhappily. *She is our treasure. We must get her off this island.*

Chapter 6

Scarlet glared out over the resort through her office window after she righted the pots that had toppled in the brief earthquake. Tyrant jumped up on the pillow she kept there and Scarlet petted her absently.

She couldn't feel Mal, which meant he wasn't at the resort, or anywhere on her half of the island.

That should be a good thing, she reminded herself. Maybe he'd packed his bags and flown home, knowing a losing battle when he faced it.

But she'd seen the amusement in his eyes, and the determination. She already knew he wasn't going to give up that easily.

Her traitor body still remembered the feeling of his hand at her waist and her fingers remembered the muscles under his dress coat.

Mal...

That was her problem. She was thinking of Mal, when she should be thinking of Mr. Moore. *Mr. Moore* was a voice on the phone that never came with good news. *Mr. Moore* was the lawyer who tried to buy the resort out from under her with drug dealers and mercenaries. *Mr. Moore* was the one making offers too good to be true for whatever nefarious purpose he clearly needed the resort for.

Mal was a different kind of problem altogether.

Tyrant reached a paw up for Scarlet's hand and extended her claws just enough to prick skin.

Scarlet obediently resumed petting her.

"I'm an idiot," Scarlet told her fiercely, then turned away. If Mal—Mr. Moore—wasn't at the resort right now, she could conduct her usual business without fear of—

Scarlet stopped herself furiously. She *wasn't* afraid.

What on earth was there to be afraid of? Mal—Mr. Moore—had no power over her. That he was here at all was an admission that all of his usual ways had failed him. The island would be hers, the resort would be hers, all of her dreams were on the brink of happening.

All of her dreams except...

Scarlet scowled and went at once to the back entrance of the kitchen, startling Darla with her approach.

The once-heiress was emptying trash into the bin, sorting out reusables, recyclables, and compost from what little would actually have to be taken to the mainland for disposal. She had a handkerchief around her strawberry-blond hair and she looked up in surprise. "I didn't hear you coming," she said, visibly alarmed and a little afraid.

Scarlet tempered her furious expression. She wasn't angry with Darla and the young woman already felt responsible for the lawsuit hanging over the resort. "I'm sorry to alarm you," she said politely. "Is Chef still in?"

"He is. They're doing some prep work for dinner." Darla looked like she was resisting the urge to curtsy, despite being covered in trash, and Scarlet strode past to go inside.

The kitchen was relatively empty; it was always busy for the catered breakfast and dinner, but midday was often quiet, with minimal wait staff attending the buffet.

Breck and Chef were merrily discussing the dinner menu.

"I don't suppose he's allergic to anything," Breck was proposing. "I wouldn't mind watching him get all puffy-faced and choke a little."

Scarlet didn't have to ask who they were talking about. "I am quite certain you are not discussing how best to poison a *guest*," she said in utterly icy tones.

They both turned and looked at her. From the way they blanched, she realized she was glowering again and she forced herself resume a serene expression.

"I'm sure I don't need to remind you that we are here to accommodate our guests, and that we will *uniformly* treat them with respect and cater to their various needs." She kept her voice level and reasonable.

Breck, who was never terribly good at hiding his feelings, looked like she'd just kicked him and she knew that she'd struck a nerve. She smothered the satisfaction it gave her to think of Mal—*Mr. Moore*—getting Breck's cold shoulder.

"I expect to receive no complaints about our level of service or the quality of our product," Scarlet said firmly, including Chef in her statement.

Even he looked chagrined.

"I assure you—" he began.

"Don't mind me," Tex sang out from the door. "I'm just going to be up here 'getting ingredients' for about an hour while Mr. Asshole Lawyer cools his heels by the—" He spotted Scarlet at that moment, and Scarlet realized that she could sense Mal—*Mr. Moore, dammit*—on the bar deck.

That he'd gotten there without her noticing bothered her almost as much noticing him now did. Scarlet slammed a fist onto the counter hard enough to make the plates rattle, but not hard enough to dent it. "You are not to harass the man!" she snarled. "I should not have to remind any of you how to be professionals!"

The kitchen, which had been quiet, went utterly silent.

Tex finally cleared his throat and someone began noisily washing dishes near the back of the kitchen. "Yes, Ma'am," the bartender said sheepishly.

"The dinner we serve him will be beyond reproach," Chef assured her.

"He shall not lack for a clean napkin or fresh water," Breck promised meekly.

Scarlet drew in a careful breath and unclenched her fist.

She was clearly overreacting.

They were all not quite looking at her and they had to recognize how unreasonable she was being. Did they think this was just because his presence meant some new bid to take the resort from her? Or did they know that she couldn't stop thinking about how he had danced with her and how his hand had felt in hers?

Scarlet kept herself from blushing with effort and cleared her throat. "Chef, I came to ask about your breakfast plans the next few days. A few of Liam's elders would like access to the kitchen one morning when the workload isn't high in order to do some baking. Mrs. Salvator's 100th birthday is coming up and they were hoping to make cupcakes."

"We can do a pancake day the day after tomorrow," Chef suggested. "That's fairly simple and will leave the ovens free."

"Very well," Scarlet said, as if she weren't helplessly imagining Mal's—Mr. Moore's—hand at her waist and the way he had smiled at her. A smug smile, she reminded herself. Which meant he thought he had the upper hand.

Which meant...

Which meant...?

Scarlet couldn't make sense of it. Why come here? What did he know that she didn't? She was scowling at Chef, she realized. "I'll inform Liam," she said, trying to pull herself together.

Everyone returned to their work and Scarlet wandered out to the restaurant before she recognized that she was unconsciously heading towards Mal like she was being drawn on a string.

She turned on her heel to leave and was caught instead by a guest who wanted to share suggestions for the amenities provided in their shower.

Chapter 7

Mal was not really expecting service at the bar when he landed there. After his experience at breakfast, he knew better than to hope for the friendly welcome that Shifting Sands had cultivated a reputation for. He was a *persona non grata* and until he had a chance to explain himself to Scarlet, he didn't expect that to change.

He wanted to find her and get this conversation out of the way, but he had to admit that he'd been shaken by his findings at Beehag's compound. A drink to settle him, and then he'd make a plan of attack. He took a beer from the cooler after the bartender's brush-off and settled into a chair near the railing that looked down over the pool.

Two giggling young women were standing near the top of the steps holding diet sodas and a short man full of attitude was trying to hold a conversation with them.

"That dragon thinks he's impressive," he was saying, nodding at the glistening green dragon acting as a lifeguard on the beach. "But pound for pound, I've got him beat with my ability to cause pain." He flexed a muscle at the nearest woman and she looked embarrassed for him. "Can you guess what I am?"

"No?" said one of the women, clearly not wanting to guess.

"Give it a shot," the man coaxed. "First one's free."

"Snake?" the other guessed with a shrug.

"Not even close," he scoffed.

"Scorpion?" the first one guessed with an ill-concealed eye-roll.

"Closer..." the man teased. When neither woman seemed interested in further speculation, he added, "People are much more terrified of me than either of those."

The women made non-committal noises and looked around for escape. Mal considered stepping in, but they only looked uncomfortable, not afraid, and now he was curious.

He didn't have to wait long.

"Fire ant," the man said smugly. "Most painful sting of any animal in the world."

The women stared.

"Do you turn into a whole swarm of them?" one asked in morbid curiosity.

The man looked confused. "Er, no."

The women exchanged amused looks and Mal could not help chuckling. While the man shot him an unappreciative look, the women escaped down the steps to the pool, their whispers and giggles trailing behind them.

Passing them on her way up was Gizelle, her hair in two untidy braids.

The fire ant shifter gave her a speculative look, but when the woman shot him a wary look and skirted along the far railing away from him in a very obvious fashion, he shrugged and went to the bar.

Mal watched Gizelle make a wide circuit of the bar, then creep around behind him. He was keenly aware of her as she circled him and finally came to stand tentatively at the table beside him. Her hands were shaking just a little.

"I remember you from the end," she said, her silky voice exactly as Mal had imagined it.

The cryptic statement cemented a suspicion that Mal had been nursing, but it didn't make him feel any better.

"You're Gizelle," Mal said gently. He was careful to keep his motions slow as he gestured to the chair. "Would you like to sit with me?"

She considered him so long that Mal was sure she was going to refuse, then, to his delight, slipped into the chair and folded herself cross-legged upon it. He had expected that it would take several tries before she trusted him enough to have a conversation.

"You're the one who sent the photographs," she said. "Tex said bad words about you and Scarlet was very angry."

She was staring hard at him and Mal thoughtfully returned her unsettling regard. "I did send the photographs," Mal admitted. "And I've discovered more about your parents since then."

Her breath caught in her throat, all of her longing bare upon her face. "Tell me..." she whispered.

Mal broke their gaze to glance around. The bartender who had gone to 'get ingredients' from the kitchen was still gone and the fire ant shifter had wandered down to the pool to try his luck with one of the sunbathers. They were, for the moment, alone on the bar deck.

"Your mother..."

"... Janine..." Gizelle sighed. "I read everything you sent. I can read now."

"Janine," Mal agreed. "She was a cockatrice shifter."

"I don't know what that is," Gizelle admitted.

"The cockatrice is a great dragon-like creature shaped a little like a bird. It has withering breath in its mythical shape, and in either form it can metaphorically turn a person to stone."

"Metaphorically?" Gizelle said sharply.

"That's when something is similar to something else, but not..." Mal started to explain.

"I know what a metaphor is," Gizelle said dismissively. "How did she turn people to stone?"

Mal found himself re-evaluating the young woman; it would be easy to assume she was simple, especially given the shy way she moved, but her gaze was sharp and knowing, if unnervingly unwavering.

"Her glance would make people afraid," Mal told her. "And with a gaze, she could trap them in their own mind, lock them away in a single memory of her choosing. Their hair would turn white and they would be like a statue, lost forever in a moment of time."

Gizelle drew in a breath, and reached for her temple, twisting her finger into one of the ivory-streaked locks.

"What was she like?" she asked plaintively.

Mal wanted to be honest with her. He wished he could reward her desperate desire for the memory of a mother to love with stories of goodness and heroism.

He thought about the lab reports he'd uncovered, the dozens of people she had destroyed in her escape, the trail of victims she'd left behind. "She was kept a long time in a laboratory, where they studied her."

"In a cage?" Gizelle said in alarm. "Like me?"

"It might as well have been a cage," Mal said carefully. "She escaped, but they chased her. And when you were young, she knew they were going to catch you."

She hadn't blinked in a long while, her brown eyes wide. "The car accident," she guessed.

"Yes. She wanted to protect you, but she wasn't able to, so she did the best thing she could for you."

"My *place*," Gizelle said knowingly, making the leap that had taken Mal months of research and dozens of spy reports to put together.

"She built a fold of time for you, so that you wouldn't have to *be* in a cage... even if she couldn't keep them from capturing you."

"Why am I not stone? Metaphorically."

Mal shrugged, and she startled back in her chair because he moved too abruptly. "I don't know how you work," he said soothingly. "I... might learn more if you showed it to me."

Gizelle knit her eyebrows together and regarded him, if possible, more intensely than before.

Was Gizelle the reason that things beneath the island were in such disrepair? Mal didn't want to believe it and certainly didn't want to think it was deliberate. But something was working at cross-purposes to him and it was possible that Gizelle's fractured magic was to blame.

He could force her to take him to that place in her mind, a few words of power and she would have to do what he told her. She was strong-willed and smart, but he was older, stronger... and wise enough to know that overpowering her would shatter the amazing progress she had made since her rescue.

Even if she was the cause of the damage he had discovered, that damage was done. Breaking her further would have only been heaping indignity on top of tragedy. Mal didn't consider the option more than the time it took to occur to him.

"I'll show you," Gizelle said at last. Before Mal could brace himself, he was falling into her eyes.

Descriptions had not prepared him.

A field of tall grass stretched in every direction, thigh-high and moving gently in a wind he couldn't feel on his skin. Everything was bright and beautiful, every blade of grass was brilliant and whispered in songs against its neighbor. Mal felt like he was bathed in sunlight, but when he looked up, squinting automatically, there was no sun and the sky was velvet black above him.

At his side, fractured from him like beams of color through a prism, was his dragon.

How curious, his dragon said, sitting up and spreading wings that cast no shadows.

Gizelle was standing before them, her hair in long, loose curls. "I made this," she said proudly. Her gazelle pranced at her side.

"Your mother made this," Mal corrected absently. "But it is from your memory." A child's memory. Incomplete.

Gizelle didn't take offense. "It is safe here, always," she said. "And I can run forever."

Mal didn't have to run for a horizon to know it would never come.

"How much time will pass, outside of here?" he asked, bending to run his fingers through the grass. He could feel each blade, but it was somehow different than physical touch.

"It depends on how wide the door is open."

"Ah..." Mal stared up at the sky. He felt like he had the pieces to several different puzzles in his hands. Puzzles with no boxes or pictures. "The door was never meant to be left open." Time was something even he didn't trifle with.

Gizelle stared. "But if the door isn't open, I can't get out."

"Your mother did that for you," Mal said, feeling as if he was on the verge of understanding something profound. "I don't know how. She wanted you to have a chance at a life outside. But *time* isn't meant to be wedged open like that. It could have... consequences."

"The rain of blood..." Gizelle murmured. "The storm... This is all my fault."

Mal scowled up at the featureless blackness above. He didn't know how things fit together yet.

"It doesn't feel right," he said, frustrated.

"I never meant to be trouble," Gizelle said as she raised her tearful gaze to Mal. She was trembling. They were sitting at the table by the bar again as all the noises of the world returned and Mal's dragon had only a moment to hiss in warning before a fist was connecting to Mal's jaw.

Chapter 8

Scarlet was beginning to suspect that the guest had a financial interest in the soaps they were trying to convince her to stock when she heard a wordless roar of rage, the sound of a punch, and then there was the crashing music of toppling chairs and tables and breaking glass.

"You must excuse me!" she called back to the guest, fleeing for the stairs.

She knew that Mal was in the thick of it, but there were people all along the way and she was concentrating so hard on getting there swiftly using her feet that she was utterly unprepared for the scene she found.

Mal was lying in the middle of a tumble of chairs and tables and broken glasses, one arm flung up over his bloodied face. Conall was holding a hysterically crying Gizelle in his arms, snarling defensively at everyone nearby. Tex was looming over Mal with a baseball bat, demanding, "What did you do to her?!" Graham, hands curled into fists, was at the far side blocking any escape and Travis was sprinting up the stairs from the pool deck.

Scarlet waded in with a snarl, flinging Tex aside with more force than she meant to. "Did I not *just* finish instructing you not to harass him? Now what the hell is going on here?"

"He wasn't hurting me," Gizelle sobbed. "He was *explaining* me."

Conall, arms wrapped firmly around her, glared at Scarlet. "She was crying," he growled without apology.

Tex, rubbing the arm that Scarlet had grabbed, sheepishly lowered his baseball bat. "I got here as Conall was landing a punch, I just assumed that Gizelle had been hassled..."

Scarlet turned to where Mal was lowering his arm. The bloody lip did not make him any less handsome, to her irritation. "*Were* you bothering Gizelle?"

"I swear I was not," he said gravely, appearing barely ruffled for all that he was looking up at her from the floor. "We were merely having... a conversation."

Scarlet glared at him, trying to assess his part in this. She had no doubts that he could have countered any attack he received; his human form was a strong as Conall or Tex's and Scarlet could not miss the dragon power that simmered beneath the surface. But he hadn't hurt either of them.

She had a chance to slight him, to make him struggle to his own feet amid the toppled furniture, and Scarlet was sorely tempted.

But she was trying to set an example of dignity, dammit, so she extended a hand to help him up.

She meant it to be just a polite assistance, quickly done, but she'd forgotten what the touch of Mal's hand did to her.

"*Mr. Moore*," she reminded herself, accidentally out loud.

"*Ms. Stanson*," he replied with an insufferable smile as he flowed to his feet and refused to let go of her hand.

"Do you require medical assistance?" she asked shortly. Tex and Travis were righting the table and chairs and sweeping up the broken bottle, but she was keenly aware of their listening ears. Graham had vanished again, at least.

Mal touched his bloody lip gingerly with his free hand and worked his jaw. "I do not," he said formally. "It should be healed in very short order. Mr. Wright has an excellent right hook." He nodded towards Conall, but the Irish elk shifter was focused entirely on Gizelle, who was beginning to calm.

Scarlet wondered if she was going to have to extract her hand using force just as he let go of it and she ground her teeth in frustration at the feeling of loss it left her with. She detested everything about this man and the way he effortlessly left her feeling like a swooning schoolgirl was the absolute worst of it.

Conall gathered Gizelle up in his arms and carried her away, murmuring to her. He shot one look of pure hatred back at Mal that made Scarlet prickle irrationally.

"I'm afraid that Mr. Wright does not appreciate my interference," Mal said regretfully.

"I'm not sure anyone appreciates your interference," Scarlet said tartly. His lip was still bloody, if not actually bleeding, and it was distracting. "You have... oh here." She stepped smartly behind the bar for a clean bar towel and wet it at the sink. "You have blood on your face," she said, holding it out to Mal, who had followed her.

He unhelpfully did not offer to take the towel and left her standing with the damp towel extended until she finally snapped, "Fine," and stepped forward to dab his jaw as efficiently as she could manage.

The worst part of it was that he knew exactly what he was doing, Scarlet thought, hating how close she had to get. She could smell his faint, heady musk, see the slight little smile at his mouth, and feel his breath against her skin. It took all of her self-control not to linger over the task.

"Thank you," Mal said quietly as she stepped back and went to rinse the towel in the sink.

He made no move to leave as she cleaned his blood from the towel and hung it to dry. "Sit with me and talk a moment," he told her, not making it a question. "I won't take much of your time."

Scarlet didn't want to give him any of her time. She only wanted him to leave her in peace and stop looking so carelessly handsome.

But he had just been *assaulted* at her resort and she was keenly aware of the curious eyes pretending not to watch them. As satisfying as giving him a cold shoulder would be, it would reflect poorly on the resort and give the staff mixed messages after her lecture about professionalism. She could have a civilized conversation with him, reiterate the uselessness of trying to talk her out of the purchase of the island, and then wash her hands of the man when he realized that his trip had been pointless.

She nodded crisply. Tex handed Mal a beer to replace the one that had been shattered and the dragon shifter took it gravely.

Scarlet led him to the far side of the bar level, above the pool, where the noise from the water features would keep their conversation private.

"I'm not sure what you hope to accomplish here," she said as they settled across the small table from each other.

"I'm hoping to convince you that the island is a poor investment choice and reconsider your offer."

"I appreciate your candor, but I am resolved to make the purchase," Scarlet replied, every bit as formally. "I have the money," she added. "And the contract dictates..."

"It's not about contracts," Mal said.

Scarlet was surprised by how passionately he said it.

He took a deep swig of his beer and looked away over the big pool. A polar bear was paddling around in the deep end and several guests in human form were lounging on pool floats at the other end. An otter was frolicking cheerfully at the base of one of the falls.

"Three hundred and fifty million dollars would buy you an island just as good," Mal said thoughtfully. "Something off of Mexico that doesn't require as much air travel, maybe. There are some properties in the Bahamas that you could get for a song compared to this."

"I think you grossly overestimate your powers of persuasion," Scarlet said coolly. "Why would I shop for another resort when I've already built exactly what I wanted?"

Mal leaned forward and looked at her intensely. His brown eyes were flecked with gold, Scarlet realized, and it took a moment for his words to register: "Because your resort isn't *safe*."

Chapter 9

If Scarlet had not been his mate, and if he had not been half in love with her before he first set eyes on her, Mal was still sure this would have been a difficult conversation.

He was used to delivering bad news and had no qualms giving hard truths to people. It was second nature to steel himself against emotional investment before all such meetings.

But Scarlet...

It wasn't just the threat of her sizzling power and it wasn't just her beauty, though both of those complicated things more than he liked to admit. He wondered if she knew exactly what she did to his body when she tucked a loose lock of hair behind her ear. The curve of her neck, the grace of her fingers, the line of her collarbone, just visible at the open neck of her blouse; it was enough to make him adjust his seat... and Mal never brought his libido to a negotiation.

It wasn't even his desire that was making it so hard to speak.

It was the vulnerability he'd glimpsed behind those flinty green eyes, the aching longing he doubted anyone else saw. He wanted to be her safety... he had never desired anything in the world so much as to be someone she could trust. He desperately wished he could tell her what she wanted to hear.

Instead, she thought he was her enemy, and he was bringing her news that would break her heart.

Scarlet narrowed her eyes. "Is this the point in our negotiations where you start threatening me?"

"No," he promised. "It's out of my hands, I swear to you. This island... it was an unfortunate place to build. It was never meant to be developed and you can't stay here much longer. I didn't realize how close to the end it was, before I came and saw for myself."

"I'm going to need more than a vague statement of doom to convince me cancel the purchase," Scarlet told him flatly. Then she gave a devastating smile, shook her head, and added, "Though I have to admit, that's a more creative angle than I was expecting."

"It's not creative," Mal protested. "I promise. Just hear me out, because benea—"

"Scarlet, I'm sorry to bother you..."

They both looked around to find Breck, looking very sorry indeed to bother them. "The cruise ship is in early with our new guests," he said apologetically. He looked at Mal warily, his tray clutched like he feared he'd have to use it as a shield.

More guests, Mal thought, his hands clenching around the beer. *More innocent shifters*.

Scarlet was standing. "We'll have to continue this conversation later," she said dismissively to Mal.

Mal stood as well. "Today," he insisted. "It's important, and we're running out of time."

For a moment, he thought she was going to refuse.

"Please," he added as an afterthought.

She pursed her lips and said reluctantly, "I should be free later this afternoon, after four."

Mal extended a hand. "At four," he said firmly.

She eyed his hand a moment before gingerly taking it and Mal savored the feeling of hers in his own. "At four, Mr. Moore," she agreed faintly, and there was that spark of uncertainty in her gaze that made him want to fold her into his arms and protect her from anything.

"Mal," he corrected. "Call me Mal."

She scowled and her eyes shuttered. "Mr. Moore," she repeated coldly and her hand was simply not in his any longer.

Her low heels clicked away over the hard tiles with a sound that Mal was already able to distinguish from anyone else and he watched her go with a smile of amusement.

Did she feel it? Did she already know that she was his mate, that he was hers, completely and utterly? Was she being coy, or simply defensive?

Alice had sworn that Scarlet wasn't a shifter; was it possible that she honestly didn't know about the bond they had? Humans supposedly felt overwhelming attraction when they met their mate, but she certainly wasn't human. Mal had seen warmth and interest in her eyes when they danced, but little of either since then. Was she denying their connection because she was angry with him, or was she truly not aware of it?

Mal realized that Breck was still standing there, watching him watch Scarlet walk away.

The waiter cleared his throat. "I owe you an apology," he said stiffly.

Mal refrained from smiling. "If you feel it necessary, I will accept your apology." Scarlet must have given him an earful. Mal sat back down.

But Breck didn't simply take his statement and go. Instead, he crossed his arms and adapted a wide-legged stance that would have looked more natural on Wrench or Graham. "Look, we all know you want the resort. But *you* should know that you won't get it without a fight. And we're all going to take it very poorly if you hurt Scarlet."

We would never hurt her, his dragon said with a hint of righteous anger. *We will protect her. At all costs.*

"I have no desire to harm Scarlet," Mal said. "And I'm sorry for the resort. I can only promise that I am not doing anything vindictively."

Breck gave a scowl that didn't suit his laughing features. "This is our home," he said fiercely. "We're not just leaving so you can make an easy buck."

Mal stared. "You think this is about money?" He gave a helpless chuckle. "If this was about money, I would not have offered Scarlet a buyout worth many times the value of the entire island."

"You offered her a buyout?" Breck looked confused.

"Several now," Mal said. "Worth millions more than your purchase offer. Didn't she tell you? She could have left the resort and bought a new place twice the size, with more amenities, or retired you all as millionaires and lived a life of luxury on some beach sipping tequila."

"*Millions* more?" Breck's look of confusion had turned to suspicion.

"All of my offers were very generous," Mal assured him. "And completely fair. No strings, no hidden agendas."

"Well you and Beehag have got some kind of agenda," Breck said, clearly not convinced. "Or you wouldn't be here, and you wouldn't have trotted those so-called businessmen through here like a slap in the face."

Mal winced. He'd begun things by trying to convince Benedict Beehag that a sale was necessary, and finding buyers he wouldn't mind watching slide into the ocean. He had hoped it would help scare Scarlet off, but she was made of sterner stuff... and once she had Jenny's help in identifying the protections set out in her contract, he realized that even an unsavory sale of the island wasn't going to convince her to break the lease.

"I can promise you that Benedict Beehag has no interest in the island whatsoever," Mal said honestly. He'd been working independently since Benedict had come whining back from one of the purchase attempts about how dangerous everything was and how crazy Scarlet was. He was currently spending his inheritance at breakneck speed through Europe with all the tail and alcohol that money could buy.

"Then why not just accept the purchase?" Breck said. "Why not just leave us in peace?"

For all of the worldliness that Breck pretended to have, he was painfully innocent.

"There are bigger things at stake," Mal said, carefully vague. He didn't want to send rumors through the staff before he was able to tell Scarlet the details himself. "Congratulations, by the way."

Breck was eyeing Mal's empty beer bottle, clearly just keeping himself from sweeping to collect it out of habit. "Congratulations for what, now?"

"Your recent nuptials," Mal reminded him. "It made waves in shifter society."

Breck gave a helpless smile. "Thank you," he said, and he rubbed his left wrist self-consciously.

"I'm pleased that my gift got to the right people," Mal couldn't help adding. "Eventually."

It didn't take Breck long to figure out what he was talking about; he was naive, but not stupid. "You gave the engagement bracelets to Darla and Liam?" Breck said in astonishment. "They were from *you*?"

"More accurately, they were from her father, who commissioned me to make them before his death."

"Why?" Breck asked avidly.

"Her father wanted her to be happy. He hoped that they would help show her the way to her own heart." Mal did not have to add that Darla's father had been desperately unhappy with his own marriage; Breck had met Darla's mother. "How are you liking the fringe benefits of my gift?"

Breck tried unsuccessfully to smother his grin. "It can be *very* entertaining."

Mal couldn't help but chuckle. "Of all the people on this island, I imagine you would be the one who could get the most enjoyment out of it."

Breck's curiosity had clearly overcome his dislike. "Did you know? When you sent these, did you know that Darla and I were mates?"

"No," Mal said with a brisk shake of his head. "I had no idea. But I knew that Liam wasn't, and I knew that Darla would somehow get to where she needed to be to meet her destiny."

"You actually believe in destiny?" Breck sounded dubious.

Mal was quiet, thoughtful. "We're all called to be in certain places, to face certain tasks. Sometimes it's not clear to us when or where or what, but shifters in particular are tuned to patterns in the world." He eyed Breck. "Would you have *chosen* to fall in love with Darla, if you'd been given a choice in the matter?"

Breck looked taken aback. "Of course not," he said, deeply reluctant. "She was promised to another. She was out of my league. She broke all my rules."

"And yet now, with her...?"

"There's no other life without her, no possible path. I never dreamed I could be so happy."

Mal nodded. "I have a theory that our animal selves can see our best possible outcome, instinctively. They recognize the pieces that take us there, even if we don't understand all the rules and can't see the full pattern."

Breck studied him. "But you think *you* do. Understand the rules. See the whole picture." His voice was full of challenge.

"More than most people, maybe," Mal said, thinking of Scarlet. He hadn't seen Scarlet coming.

We have always known that our destiny was at this island, his dragon assured him confidently.

But Mal's vision of that destiny had been glorious battle, victory over a terrible threat to the world. It hadn't involved a woman with eyes that looked straight into his soul, or the ferocious desire that rose in him every time he caught sight of her. His whole understanding of his fate had been turned on its head.

He finished the last swig of his beer and handed the bottle to Breck, who put it on his tray with a practiced flair.

"Shifting Sands might surprise you," the waiter said in unexpected echo to his own thoughts. "It might even teach you something about yourself. It has a habit of doing that."

Mal thought it just might.

Chapter 10

Scarlet checked in the new guests personally, as she usually did. It was the usual mix: dilettantes who spent money like water, couples who were celebrating anniversaries or honeymoons, middle class people who had carefully saved up for the vacation of a lifetime. She confirmed the rules with each of them, gathered signatures for all the various forms, and gave them keys.

Usually, this was one of her favorite things to do. It was pleasant to meet new people, to see the shining anticipation in their faces, to watch how they reacted to the amenities and activities she described to them. They took deep breaths of the island air and marveled at the smells and delighted in the architecture and Scarlet felt a sense of deep accomplishment and pride.

But today she could not help but think of Mal's statement: *Your resort isn't safe.*

What did he mean by that? Was this just lawyer talk? He seemed sincere. Insufferably smug, yes, but when he'd talked to her, he seemed genuinely concerned.

Concerned and... interested.

His eyes haunted her, so warm and fearless.

Their conversations on the phone had prepared her for someone cool and logical. But Mal—Mr. Moore—had an expressive face and Scarlet had caught a dozen emotions there in the space of a conversation. She found this very unnerving.

That, and she had expected someone old. Jenny said he'd been practicing law since the sixties, which meant he had to be at least eighty.

"Which room number?"

"Eighty..." Scarlet said, distracted. She shook herself. "I mean, that will be 215 in the hotel. You have a lovely view from that floor."

The guest smiled gratefully and Scarlet made herself concentrate on the transaction and show her the map. "My staff has already delivered your luggage, no need to worry."

"Thank you so much!"

Scarlet shut down the computer after the guest took their over-sized purse and left the courtyard and stared at her dark reflection in the screen for a moment. It wasn't like she should judge Mal for looking younger than he was. She closed the laptop firmly.

The resort outside the courtyard was filled with the noises of new guests, people exclaiming over the beauty and thoughtfulness of the layout, loudly asking for directions, greeting the people they'd gotten to know on the cruise. Some of them went directly for the bar, where there was already happy chatter despite the early hour.

Your resort isn't safe.

Scarlet scowled over her domain. *Mr. Moore* had some explaining to do.

She stalked to the spa, where several guests were already gathered around the board that described the various services available.

"Oh, I'm definitely up for a massage," a young woman was saying.

"But what kind?" the older woman with her asked eagerly. "I don't even know what some of these *are*!"

Scarlet slipped past them to catch Lydia settling clean sheets over the massage tables.

"I wanted to give you heads up about a guest with a coconut allergy, a Mrs. Orainda Santaga."

Lydia finished tucking the corners under and went to write down the allergy on her scheduling sheet. "Thank you, Scarlet. Did we get many guests from the cruise ship?"

"About a dozen," Scarlet said.

"Oh good, we should be set for hands in the spa for today without calling Laura in." Lydia suddenly looked very cagey, an unnatural look for her, and added, "She wasn't feeling well earlier today, poor thing."

Scarlet, who already knew about Laura's pregnant condition but was letting everyone think she didn't, had to keep an amused smile from her face with effort as Lydia bustled to find an alternate oil for the woman with the coconut allergy.

She caught sight of her reflection in one of the many mirrors and gave her serene face some thoughtful consideration.

Was she looking dated? Her clothing was the type generally called *timeless*, but maybe it was *past* time to try something new. And her hair, was it too severe? She touched the bun that always pulled her bright hair back from her face and wondered if it seemed uninviting.

A scowl reflected back at her. She didn't want to look inviting and she was certainly not going to change her look because some stuck-up, big-shot lawyer from the city had come to her resort and danced with her.

Scarlet was furious with herself.

She rolled her shoulders back firmly and went to the kitchen to deliver the coconut allergy warning to Chef personally as well.

She *hated* Mal Moore, she reminded herself. He was her *enemy*.

Chapter 11

There was a young cat on Scarlet's windowsill, grooming itself with one green eye firmly on Mal.

Mal had never considered that Scarlet would be the kind of person to have a pet and the creature was rather confounding.

He should probably attempt to win it over; the best way to exert influence was sometimes sideways. He stood on the far side of Scarlet's desk trying to figure out how to achieve this goal. "Nice, kitty," he attempted. "Come."

The cat continued to twist itself in an impressive display of flexibility and run its tongue over its short, plush fur vigorously. It clearly had no intention of obeying.

It is very... small, his dragon observed. *What purpose does it serve? Is she raising it to eat?*

Don't eat it, Mal said firmly. He was sure that would not improve his relationship with Scarlet.

He went around the desk to stand near it, since it was clearly not well-trained. Food was not the worst idea that his dragon had ever had. Perhaps it could be tempted with a treat. "What do cats eat?" He knew a little about dogs, but his exposure to cats was limited to media, and *limited* was the appropriate word for it.

His dragon gave a mental shrug. *Mice?*

Mal was strongly dubious that Scarlet would allow roaming mice at the resort. Unless they were guests.

The cat appeared to have finished its licking and now stared up at him, unblinking. After a moment of contemplation, it gave a trilling half-purr. Mal extended a hand to pet it and, alarmingly, it fell over on its side and rolled to its back.

Had he frightened it? It extended its legs, four limbs in each direction, and writhed in place as it made more of its trilling noises. Its belly was soft-looking and fluffy. Clearly this was an invitation for affection.

"It's a trap," Scarlet said from behind him.

Mal, alarmed that he hadn't heard her approach, let his hand fall carelessly to the young cat's belly.

The cat instantly curled into itself and reached up with all four paws, wrapping itself around Mal's forearm with suddenly extended claws. Sharp teeth gnawed at his wrist, hard enough that he felt the prick through his shirt sleeve, but not quite hard enough to draw blood.

Mal bit back a yelp of surprise and forced himself not to fling the little monster; it was clearly young and just as clearly playing; once he'd gotten past the shock of the attack he recognized that it hadn't caused any real pain, even when it kicked out with its rear feet.

Ah, his dragon said. *Our mate is raising it as a guardian.*

Mal was pretty sure she didn't need one.

"Hsst, Tyrant," Scarlet said, sounding amused. "She's only playing," she explained to Mal.

Tyrant—fittingly named—gave Mal one final gnaw and then let go. Ears back against her head, she leapt for the floor, raced under the desk, and streaked out into the courtyard, nearly crashing into the door frame as her paws scrabbled on the hard tile.

"She's a feisty thing," Mal observed.

"You were going to explain why my resort is in terrible peril," Scarlet reminded him. "And I was going to decide if I should believe you."

Mal came around the desk so that he was standing close to her, breathing in the green scent of her, enraptured by the marble perfection of her pale skin and the fiery strands of her gleaming hair. Her eyelashes were coal black over her endless eyes.

"Scarlet Stanson," he said after a moment. "Aaric Lyons' secretary."

"That was a long time ago," Scarlet said coldly.

"Do you know, there was a while I suspected you were an impersonator. I thought you'd hacked the Lyons' account, found the lease contract, and decided it would be convenient to pretend to be the only person with the power to re-open the resort. For a short time, I even thought you might be working with Alistair Beehag, to supply him with rare shifters for his zoo."

Her cool mask cracked to hot fury. "I would *never*—"

"I know," Mal said swiftly. "That theory didn't last much longer than the others that I had. But it *was* a surprise to find out you weren't a shifter," he said softly. "It raised so many questions."

"Alice might have been lying," Scarlet suggested, confirming that she knew about Alice's deal with Mal. "Or maybe she just got the wrong information. Perhaps even on purpose..."

Mal laughed. Her misdirection was convincing, but: "I know you're not a shifter."

"How can you be so sure?" Scarlet asked.

"If you were a shifter, you would have recognized me as your mate when we met."

Her entire face changed, melting into astonishment and wonder as her lips parted in shock. "Your... mate?" Her voice was full of longing, and she seemed to hear herself and drew back a step. "I don't know what kind of joke this is..."

"That's not something I would joke about," he told her. He closed the distance between them with a decisive step. "Scarlet..."

She tipped her face up to gaze at him in confusion and desire and didn't pull back as he cupped her jaw and bent to kiss her.

For a moment, she was stone against his lips, then he tasted a wistful sigh and she was opening her mouth to kiss him back.

Her arms slipped up around him and he pulled her close against him, twining fingers into her upswept hair. He didn't feel any pins, but he must have dislodged them, because her hair was suddenly alive around them.

She was all the wildness and strength she promised, all the untamed passion he'd known lurked behind her icy control. She was desperate and hungry and she was his.

She was *his*.

Mal had never felt such joy and satisfaction and aching need. She would come safely away from the island with him and he would worship her for the rest of their long lives.

He would never be alone again...

He lifted her to the top of her desk, hands at her waist, and a pile of papers tilted and slipped off the back of the desk.

Scarlet didn't seem to care.

She was pushing his shirt off his shoulders, hands caressing down his arms as she bared them. The cuffs were buttoned too tight to slip from his wrists so she was thwarted above his elbows, but she was busy using her fingers to explore, wandering across his chest as they kissed again, desperately and deeply.

He had one hand up under her skirt exploring the plane of her thigh, one at her neck, and her skin was every bit as silky as he'd imagined it must be. He needed her, like he'd never needed anything, and triumph rose in his chest because finally, *finally*... The months they'd sparred, the phone calls, the letters... it was like the longest foreplay in the world.

And now they would have forever.

Forever, he thought, then he realized in shock that his hand had reached her hip and not found the line of underwear he was expecting. He laughed into her kiss, delighted and amused as his fingers walked over her perfect thigh to verify the shocking truth: she wasn't wearing undergarments.

Conservatively dressed, fiercely independent, perfectly put together Scarlet Stanson was completely naked under her modest skirt. And when he touched her clit, carefully and gently, she gave a whimper of desire and spread her legs for him, tearing at his shirt, desperately seeking his skin.

Yes, his dragon purred. *Ours...*

Mal had only a split second to recognize Scarlet's hand, flat on his chest, before he was smashing into the opposite wall, hard enough to rattle every book on the shelves.

He was confused, blinking at Scarlet, and his dragon mantled his wings in surprise. Hadn't he managed to get a few of her buttons undone? But she was fully dressed again, bearing down on him from across the room, and even her hair was neatly back in its bun. She was somehow larger and the air in the room felt hard to breathe.

"How dare you!" she snarled. "Was this your plan all along? Did you think you could bind my people? Did you think you could *seduce* me into complacency and steal them from under my nose? Is this why you wanted the resort so *badly*?"

Mal stared, still not making sense of how everything had changed so completely in so little time. This felt like much more than just moving too fast... then he realized that Scarlet had gotten one of his sleeves off—who knows where the buttons had gone—and the runic tattoos that swirled down his left forearm were clearly visible.

Her sole experience with warlock tattoos would have been Corbin, who stole shifters and bound them to drain their magical energy.

"Scarlet—"

"You won't get a single one of them without going through me," she hissed. "And good luck with that!"

The vines that were draped around the room had come to life and were snaking down from every direction to twist around his wrists and ankles and neck. He tore free from one to find another, and another, swiftly unfurling new growth at him.

"I'm not here for them," he protested.

"Me, then?" Scarlet was standing at arm's length, and Mal didn't think he imagined the fact that she was taller now, looking him straight in the eyes with blazing anger. "Did you think you could bind *me*?"

"Scarlet, wait—" Mal was trying to unbutton his remaining sleeve, but the vines and the pressure of magic in the room were making it a struggle. He muttered a quick incantation and the buttons burst from the sleeve so that he could slip it off. "I don't need to bind anyone," he insisted, holding up his right forearm. "I'm a dragon shifter, my own power is more than sufficient."

Scarlet paused as the runes on both of his arms, now exposed, flared with brief light, and the air seemed a little less thick.

Mal used her moment of hesitation to rip free of the vines and close the distance between them.

"Corbin and his cronies used a terrible perversion of ancient dragon magic. If the Phoenix had not taken care of them, I would have done so personally. Your guests—*your* people—have nothing to fear from me."

"So it's only *me* that you've got some sort of vendetta against," Scarlet hissed.

Mal drew a deep breath for patience and it seemed less dense. The vines still whispered threateningly behind and above him, but didn't move to try to restrain him again. "I don't have a vendetta," he said firmly. "But I can explain, if you'd just *listen*."

"I'm not leaving the island," Scarlet insisted. "You can't frighten me, and you can't fool me."

"Dammit, Scarlet," Mal said, letting all of his frustration show. "Stop being so stubborn. Listen and judge for yourself. Sit down with me and let me tell you what I know. Please."

The anger seemed to have leaked out of her, leaving only wariness. "Fine," she said, after a moment of silence. "*Outside.*"

A door from her office led to a tidy, sparsely decorated bedroom with sliding glass doors that opened onto a small, private lawn with a round table and two chairs. Mal took one sideways look at the bed as they passed through, wishing things had gone a different way.

Soon, his dragon growled. *She cannot resist us long, and we will take her safely from this place.*

Chapter 12

The sun was still high in the sky, a blazing coin above them in a bright blue sky. It was baking hot on Scarlet's lawn, though the worst of the afternoon heat was past.

She should have made him put his shirt back on, missing buttons or not, Scarlet thought as she settled into one of the chairs. His chest was terribly distracting and she scowled to think how easily he had weaseled his way through her defenses.

He *wasn't* her mate. That could only be another half-truth to wear her down. He hadn't actually said he was her mate, had he? Only that if she were a shifter she'd have known he *was* her mate... there was surely some sort of lawyer loophole there. She'd been a fool to let him kiss her, too surprised, too full of longing and desire to be sensible.

He clearly knew her greatest weakness. She needed to keep more distance, be more careful, and shut down her instincts more thoroughly.

And his bare chest was suggesting that the table between them was not nearly wide enough for the distance she needed. She couldn't stop replaying his kiss, his words, the feeling of his hands over her skin...

"What do you have to tell me?" she demanded, furious with herself for continuing to let him bait her with his sexual appeal.

"I'm a dragon shifter," Mal said, and he raised his arms to her in demonstration. "A warlock dragon from a long proud line going back for thousands of years. Our magic has quietly been keeping order between shifters and humans... and other things... for centuries."

"Other things..." Scarlet said suspiciously.

"There are old things in the world. Older than people. Older than dragons. And one of those things sleeps beneath this island."

Did he think she would be surprised by this revelation? "I know of this creature," she said cautiously. "It has never bothered me or mine." She could not help adding, "Which is more than I can say about you."

"I have never tried to destroy the world," Mal retorted. "And if—when—it wakes, it will attempt to take a vengeance that will drown not just this island, but all islands, and all continents, and it will not rest until the world has been ravaged."

Scarlet scowled at him skeptically, but she was listening carefully. "What *is* it?"

"It is a great wyrm with two heads, covered in deadly sharp feathers. It can appear as a human, but don't be deceived. It is not a *shifter*, it is a powerful, old creature of air and water and it is wrathful. It is instinct and anger, not reason. It is wild, and vicious... and it's going to be really pissed off when it wakes up."

"You're saying this thing is just... napping beneath my island?"

"Not just sleeping, but imprisoned as well; my family is thorough. Eleven hundred years ago, my great-grandfather battled him into submission and built a cage around him deep beneath the island."

"Why not just kill him?" Scarlet asked. "Wouldn't that have been simpler?"

"It is immortal. There is no way to *kill* it because it's not really alive. Imprisonment was the only choice. Every three hundred years, the spells are renewed, the cage is rebuilt, and the wyrm is cast down again. My grandfather did so the second time, and then my father, almost two hundred years ago."

"And now it's your turn?" Scarlet wrenched her eyes up from his damned chest and scowled, trying to make herself focus. "That math doesn't add up."

Mal's eyes were no less distracting than his muscle-knotted shoulders. "We should have decades more, but we don't. I don't understand what has happened, but the cage is crumbling, and its slumber has been disturbed."

"Corbin?" Scarlet proposed. "Gizelle said he was... noisy."

"He might have precipitated the creature waking, but I don't understand the damage to the cage that I've seen. It's less recent, more insidious. It's as if it has slowly rusted... the magic feels old and weak, and it's leaked into all of the rock around it." If Mal full of confidence was devastating to Scarlet's peace of mind, Mal admitting that he didn't know something was even more unsettling. He raked a hand through his hair and gave a confused shrug. "I checked the wyrm's prison myself when Rupert Beehag began construction and it was as strong and impenetrable as ever at that time. There's been some change, something new since then. I thought it might be Gizelle's broken magic... but it could just as easily be *you*."

Scarlet drew in her breath with a hiss. "You think *I* did this?"

Mal met her gaze without flinching. "I don't know what you are," he reminded her. "I don't know how you work. But since *you* came here, a spell that previously withstood hundreds of years containing the power of creature older than the continents has crumbled to almost nothing in the span of a few decades."

Scarlet stared back at him, more dismayed than she wanted him to know.

"I don't think you necessarily did anything on purpose," Mal added swiftly. "I know you well enough to know that you aren't trying to release an old thing to destroy or rule the world. Maybe this has happened because of some aspect of what you are. Or some side effect of something you're *doing* here. If I knew more about your nature..."

This could be *her* fault? Scarlet almost drowned in the guilt that rose in her throat.

Mal leaned forward onto his elbows, which made all the planes of his shoulders change in a terribly distracting way.

"You were never my enemy, Scarlet," he said.

"You certainly never treated me like an ally," Scarlet retorted sharply. "If you needed me to leave so badly, why didn't you come tell me all this in the first place?"

"Would you have gone? Would you have believed me?" Mal countered. "Until I saw the radar maps of the storms this week, I thought I had plenty of time to solve this puzzle—years if not decades. I had no idea that Corbin would do anything so stupid as start to wake the creature up, and I didn't realize that the cage was failing until I got here. I thought I could play the long game, and I could apply just enough pressure that you would do what was best... best for *you*... without having to step in and force your hand."

"Is that what this is to you?" Scarlet asked scathingly. "A *game*? Where *you* are the superior chessmaster sitting back in his throne dictating the lives of those less worthy?"

"No," Mal said at once. Then, hesitantly, "Maybe." He raked his hand through his hair again and Scarlet had to glare at her hands to stop herself from staring at his chest. She really should have made him put that shirt back on.

"I'm sorry," he said, so unexpectedly that Scarlet had to look at him again. She nearly drowned in his intense golden-brown eyes. "I played this whole situation poorly and if I had it to do over, I would have done things very differently. I made assumptions I never should have made. I expected you to..."

"...Roll over and take gobs of money to move somewhere else like a good little game piece." Scarlet laughed humorlessly. "And I was having none of that."

She tried to focus on the larger problem. "Can you make the cage again, from scratch? Can you set the spell again, but early? Do you have that power?"

"Of course," Mal said with maddening confidence. "I have trained all of my life for it, and have all the power and knowledge necessary. But doing so will wake the wyrm. I will have to fight him into submission to build the cage around him and that will raze the island. There was not a tree left standing here after the last battle."

Scarlet could not quite keep the noise of dismay from escaping her pursed lips.

"That, *that,* is why I have been trying to get you to release the resort. I thought I had plenty of time until I got here, but the end result was always going to be the same. The island will certainly be destroyed and everyone still on it will die."

The look of sympathy in his eyes was both unwelcome and unnerving. "I understand that you built this place with Aaric Lyons and that you have some debt to him that you feel compels you to continue his dream. I know that this resort is your calling and that your hard work and perseverance has seen it to fruition. And I admire that, Scarlet. I admire *you*. This place you've built is impressive, and you've done it against incredible odds... myself included. You don't want my charity, that's fine, I more than respect that. So take the three-hundred-fifty million you raised by yourself. Go buy a beautiful new island and build a better resort. I'll fight my fight, reset the spells, and the last of Beehag's terrible zoo will crumble to dust and slide into the sea. Everyone will live happily ever after. You have to see why this is the only path ahead."

Scarlet stood and paced away to the edge of the lawn, staring over the resort to the ocean with her arms wrapped around herself.

She didn't want to believe him, and she didn't want to trust him. But everything Mal said rang true, and everything matched the things she already knew. She'd felt the creature below the island, and knew its wild power, even if she didn't understand what it was or where it had come from. She had always known, instinctively, that to wake it would spell disaster.

And Mal...

She'd spent so long hating him that she had a hollow place in her chest where that anger had burned, and it felt raw and tender inside... and that frightened her more than her fury ever had.

Was he really her mate? Yearning threatened to swamp her logical thought and she forced the question away. It had no bearing here.

What mattered were the people who trusted her, all the shifters at the resort who didn't know the danger they were in: her guests, her staff... her friends.

"How long?" she asked, not turning. "How long do we have?"

She heard Mal rise and cross the lawn to her. "Not long. The storms that will make landfall in a few days are his doing. He has control over wind and water and my gut says that they aren't a coincidence. His method of destruction will be storms and floods of a scope humans have never seen and have no defense against. He will make our category fives look like child's play. Storm surge will reach your office."

She looked down the long, steep slope over the roofs of the cottages, the waving treetops, and the glittering pool. The ocean looked peaceful, far below.

"When he wakes, the cage won't be able to withstand him in its current state." Mal hesitated. "Scarlet, I have to stop him if that happens. I *have* to battle him down and reset the spell *at that moment,* before he breaks free... it wouldn't matter who was here, who got killed in the crossfire. I can fight him in his resting place, but if he breaks free, he's in his element of strength and I'm at a disadvantage. And if he gets loose on the world, it would be so much worse. I don't know who could stop him, or how long it would take, and how many he would kill first. You have to believe me, Scarlet. You have to leave. You have to leave *now.*"

Scarlet turned to him. "I believe you," she said quietly. "I don't *want* to believe you, but I do."

His eyes were full of sympathy she didn't want... and he didn't even understand the scope of what he was telling her.

"It's late and the storms are a few days out. I'll start the evacuation tomorrow morning. I need to make some phone calls, we'll get the air charter out here as many times as they can schedule. The storms at least are real, we can use them as our reason for the exodus." She paced to the table and pushed the chairs in neatly, as if arranging the furniture would somehow make everything better.

"I know someone who can put a few news articles up to support the story," Mal offered. "A general widespread evacuation warning of the coast in this area might look more likely than just a single island."

"I'll have Jenny cancel the purchase and return the funds they raised. But..." Scarlet looked at Mal and swallowed her pride with effort. "You offered me a buyout. I know I refused it. But if it's still on the table, I want it. I want the staff to be able to retire comfortably. They deserve that."

"I offered you three buyouts," Mal said dryly. "Every one of them generous by any measure. But why not start the resort again somewhere else? Your people would follow you anywhere and you *have* the funds."

Scarlet smiled at him, a slow, sad smile. "*I* can't leave the island."

"I know it means a lot to you..."

She reached out and touched his face, because he was standing so close, and because he was so handsome that she couldn't resist it. "I *can't* leave the island," she repeated with emphasis. She took her hand back before she was tempted to do more. "It didn't matter how much money you offered me, or how much pressure you put on me... leaving the island was never an *option* for me."

Mal scowled at her. "I don't understand. Is it a magical compulsion? I can break those."

Scarlet shook her head slowly.

"A contract?" Mal's voice took on a hint of alarm as the ramifications of what she was telling him sunk in. "I'm arguably one of the best lawyers in the world. I could get you out of anything."

"Modest, too," Scarlet observed wryly. "The only contracts binding me are the ones you already know about."

"Then *what*? Scarlet, you *can't* be here when this goes down!" He sounded angry, but Scarlet heard the note of panic in his voice.

Scarlet lifted her chin and smoothed down her skirt. "I'll show you," she decided finally. "Come with me."

"Show me what?" Mal scrambled to follow.

Scarlet shot him a look over her shoulder as she led him back through her office. "What I really am." She pointed to his shirt, slumped on the floor. "Put your shirt on."

Chapter 13

Mal suspected he'd appreciate Scarlet's suggestion to wear his shirt; the buttons at the wrists were gone, but he solved this indignity by rolling up his sleeves, walking fast to catch Scarlet. To his surprise, she did not pause at her office door, or head down into the resort, but led him out of the courtyard, past the entrance, along the low stone wall, and then plunged into the jungle before him.

Scarlet moved swiftly through the trees before him, flitting ahead as easily as if she was on a paved walk. Mal had glimpses of her ahead, as he clamored over roots and pushed aside leaves the size of tables to follow. Her skirt, which had seemed so conservative in her office—lack of undergarments aside—was hiked up above her knees and her long, pale legs flashed in the deepening green shadows.

At one point, Mal was astonished to realize that she was still wearing her modestly-heeled shoes, over ground that even he found challenging in flat dress shoes... and that he still seemed to hear the distinctive click that they made over tile.

Before he could reconcile this oddity, he was breaking out of the clinging shadows into an unexpected clearing. The sun was beginning to set; the sky above them was stained purple and gold in the hole of the jungle canopy above.

For a moment, Mal thought that Scarlet's true form was too big to show him in a constrained space and she'd brought him here for privacy.

Then he realized that the clearing wasn't empty.

In the center of the jungle-ringed space was a tree.

Mal was no arborist, but even he could tell at once that this was no ordinary tree. It wasn't that impressive in size, compared to the gigantic trees of the jungle surrounding them, but it was still grand, as big as a house, with thick fern-like leaves and a heavy crown of brilliant red flowers.

Mal didn't have to cast his power sight to know that it sizzled with power: power like Scarlet's.

And it had brilliant red flowers: red like Scarlet's hair.

She was watching him with something that might have been anxiousness in a lesser person.

"This is me," she said needlessly, because Mal had put all the pieces of this puzzle together at last. "This is why I can never leave the island."

"You're a dryad," he said in wonder.

Dryads were a Greek myth, but similar stories existed in many cultures: a powerful nature spirit who was anchored to a single tree, guardian of her forest and land.

"This is my tree," she said simply. "This is my forest. This is my island."

They had closed the distance to the tree and the branches bent down in greeting.

Mal reached up and ran his fingers through the feathery leaves. They curled around his fingers and stroked his arms curiously.

Scarlet gave a little sigh, and Mal turned to see her eyes half-closed in pleasure.

"It has been a long time since anyone really touched me," she said achingly.

Questions crowded in Mal's mouth: how did she grow here? What was her connection with the Lyons? How did her stunning power *work*?

And most critical: how could he protect her from the devastation of rebuilding the wyrm's prison? Letting the island become a battleground was no longer a palatable option... but it had always been the *only* option.

We cannot let her come to harm, his dragon wailed. *But we cannot fail our destiny!*

"I have photographs of you in England, from the sixties," Mal said, confused. "You had brown hair."

"Royal poinciana doesn't bloom in England," Scarlet said, as if it made perfect sense. She reached up and caressed some of the leaves; they twined around her fingers. "It only thrives in the tropics."

"But... you were *in* England. How...?"

"I woke up there. Probably a traveler brought a seed pod back from a vacation; I only know that I woke up when I was a sapling in a pot. I was root bound, starting to die, so I picked up my pot and went looking for someone to help me. I found the lot with the happiest trees and went to ask them to save me."

While Scarlet spoke, she sat down in the thick moss beneath her tree, and the ground beneath her raised into a mossy root chair that conformed to her shape and cradled her like a throne. Apparently, she was done hiding her abilities from him and the analyst in him desperately wanted to test what she could do.

He didn't doubt she could raise the entire jungle onto its roots and march it forward in battle, if it came down to it. Could she use her power to protect the island while he battled the wyrm? Already, his mind was churning through possible solutions.

Mal sat carefully across from her, mimicking her motion, and was unnerved by the sensation of the roots beneath the springy moss rearranging themselves and lifting him into a chair.

"That lot, as you've probably guessed, belonged to Aaric Lyons, who was in the midst of preparing for his wedding."

"To Coral Jennings," Mal said, recalling his research.

"No, actually," Scarlet gave a tiny, conflicted smile. "He was engaged to Rupert Beehag's daughter, Anna. Coral was a landscaper who was there to do the finishing touches on the grounds for the ceremony. He took me to find her for advice on my tree... and met his mate. He had hired her by phone, and that was the first time they'd seen each other..."

Scarlet was avoiding his gaze, finding anything else to look at. Mal wanted to reach for her, badly, and his dragon was grumbling impatiently inside. He waited.

"They were very kind to me. I had nothing but a pot with a dying tropical tree in it and Aaric had me re-potted, took me into his household, taught me how to blend in, educated me, and eventually built a glass greenhouse where I lived for nearly twenty years. Then, he bought half of a tropical island and paid an exorbitant amount of money to have me freighted across the world and planted here."

She pursed her lips, then went on evenly. "It wasn't an easy road for them. She was from a poor area where shifters were being harassed and he was a young lord who was expected to make a brilliant match with an influential businessman's daughter. Aaric chose to break off the engagement at the last moment and marry Coral."

She shook her head. "It was messy. Anna was already pregnant—not by Aaric, but I think her father was hoping that her marriage to him would hide the shame, and instead, it became very public and ugly. I thought that Rupert Beehag took the disgrace very well; they continued business arrangements, and even made the purchase of this island together. But it's clear he never forgave Aaric and, it appears, grew to hate shifters."

Scarlet balled fists at her side.

"When Aaric vanished, the resort was almost finished, but it was discovered that he had been in financial straits. I wonder now, if Rupert didn't play a large role in that, as well. The workers all quit and left, and Coral... Coral was devastated. She knew that Aaric was dead, even if she didn't have any proof. She wanted to take their son to England, where she thought they would be safe, and *Rupert,* her good friend *Rupert,* made a very generous offer to buy her half of the island, leaving the option open to buy it back whenever she, or her heirs, could. It was quicker than a loan, and the contract looked ironclad. Rupert didn't know what I was, of course... I was just Aaric's secretary on paper, he had no idea I was tethered to the island. Coral... she thought she'd come back quickly, that it would take a few years at the most to figure out what had gone wrong with the bookkeeping and get it all fixed. A few years isn't so long for a dryad."

"She never came back," Mal finished for her.

"I found out, decades later, that she died in a car accident, shortly after returning to England. Her son received a life insurance settlement that got him on his feet again, but he was just a kid, and he only knew me as an eccentric aunt. He had problems of his own, without wondering what had happened to me or worrying about some island he barely remembered. He got married, had a son... died a pauper. I didn't know any of that... I was just... waiting."

"For almost forty years."

"Until cell phone coverage reached the island and I could communicate with the rest of the world again."

"*That's* why you were missing for so long." Mal whistled. "You were actually *here* the whole time." *Alone*, Mal thought. *Alone on an island of your broken hopes.*

"If you tell me I look good for my age, I will throw you off my island, reservation or not." That was the Scarlet he knew so well, full of spice.

"I wouldn't dream of it," Mal said honestly. "My compliments are much more clever than that."

"I wouldn't know," Scarlet said dryly. "The last time we spoke on the phone, I believe you called me a stubborn harpy who wouldn't understand a smart deal if it bit me in the ass."

For a moment Mal could only smile at her, bemused. "I had offered you twice the value of the island and a reasonable settlement on Jubilee Grant's lawsuit simply to sever the lease. What else was I supposed to assume?"

"Maybe you shouldn't make assumptions," Scarlet said sharply.

She rose from her chair and paced away. The moss chair melted back into the earth. Mal rose and followed her.

The tree above them shuddered and Scarlet shut her eyes. "I found Aaric's hide in Alistair's study, after we freed the zoo. There was a short time there, after his death, where the contract hadn't been passed to Benedict yet and I could go there."

"You were there when the zoo was freed," Mal remembered.

"I made Jimmy invite me," Scarlet hissed. "I was extremely persuasive. The contract allowed me to visit, though I could feel it dampening my power."

Mal could feel her fury and helplessness. He remembered puzzling over the weirdly detailed specifications in the resort lease and the older contract that dictated rights of first sale. "The Beehags have always been very good at hiding their true nature," he growled, remembering how betrayed he'd felt when he discovered what was happening at their compound.

"I still feel like I should have known what was happening," Scarlet said quietly, bowing her head. The wind in the branches gave a sorrowful sigh.

"The contract..."

"The contract was written to protect the shifters at Shifting Sands... and to protect *me*. None of us ever dreamed that Rupert and later his grandson would use it conceal something like... *that*."

The sun was almost down now, the sky velvet indigo overhead. A silver moon, nearly full, cast crisp, cool light over the clearing, and in the shadows under Scarlet's tree it was growing dark. Mal could see in the dark, thanks to his dragon, but it was almost colorless sight; Scarlet's hair, and the flowers in the tree, had lost their red hue.

Her eyes were still emerald when she turned to look at him, luminescent to his sight, and Mal felt like he was looking straight down to the center of her, to all of her years of loneliness, all of her strength, and every regret.

She was so beautiful, so complicated.

"I wish I had done something sooner, stopped him..."

"It wasn't your fault," Mal interjected.

"I could have..." she spread her hands helplessly.

"You did everything you could. More than you had to." Mal had kept his hands from her longer than he'd thought possible and he failed to resist the urge to comfort her where he'd been able to resist touching her for his own pleasure. She didn't pull away when he took her hands, and when he drew her close, she didn't protest, merely looked at him with those glowing eyes.

He didn't kiss her, though he desperately wanted to, only opened his arms and gathered her into a tight embrace. He held her close and, after a moment, she sighed and put her arms around him.

Chapter 14

Scarlet leaned into Mal's body, trying to absorb his strength and comfort. She was so filled with yearning and emotion that she didn't know what to do with any of it. She hadn't spoken of Aaric or her guilt over Beehag's zoo to anyone, bottling it up as deeply as she could manage.

Her trust of Mal was alarming in its intensity. His motives were clear now and all of their past strife had logical, if misguided, explanations once they'd bothered to sit down and untangle the underlying confusion.

It felt amazing not to have secrets, for the first time in such a long time... almost as amazing as it felt to have strong arms around her, holding her close.

Scarlet could not help but remember his gaze—amused and full of wonder—as he told her why he knew she wasn't a shifter.

Her *mate*. Was it true?

It was impossible not to realize he wanted her; he was trying not to press his erection against her, but Scarlet was not oblivious to its hardness between them, or the way his fingers kept caressing her and stopping as if the desire was rising in him like it was in her and he wasn't sure what to do with it.

"We never finished our dance," he murmured near her ear.

"That's a shame," she whispered back. "But I suppose we still could..."

With small adjustments, one hand was in hers and one was at the small of her back, and they were no less close as Scarlet walked her fingers to his shoulder, wishing now that she *hadn't* encouraged him to put his shirt back on. The runes on his forearms gleamed slightly in the darkness below his rolled-up sleeves.

She smoothed the mossy ground to a seamless flat dance floor and when he led her out into a slow, sensual salsa set to the sounds of the jungle at night, she let herself close her eyes and melt into him the way she had been dying to when he first danced with her.

This time, he did dip her, and she rose back up to the unheard music that they were dancing to and pressed her mouth against his, too hungry to resist any longer.

They made love slowly this time, the frantic need they felt tempered with the will to prolong every touch, every caress, every discovery they made of each other.

Scarlet drew a fingernail curiously along his runes as she pulled his shirt off of him for a second time and he hissed and yanked too hard on one of her blouse buttons. She forced herself to be patient and let him remove every piece of clothing and was rewarded with careful kisses that made her whimper in anticipation.

Mal slipped off his shoes without untying them and when they were finally naked together, he kissed her again and again, and it was even more glorious without anything keeping their moonlit skin apart.

He laid her down onto the moss—she made a thick, moss-soft bed for them without more than a thought for it—and she spread her legs for him eagerly.

Mal teased her, pressing but not entering, until she was begging him without words, scratching his shoulder and tugging at his strong arms and arching up to thrust herself at him in desperation.

When he finally slid into her, she was wet and more than ready and her world exploded into light. He brought her wave after wave of pleasure, every thrust a crest, every kiss a surrender, and Scarlet felt as if her heart would give out from sheer joy.

He finally gave a cry of release and cradled her through their aftershocks as he succumbed to his own need at last.

They lay tangled together as Scarlet remembered to breathe again and Mal's heartbeat returned to something more normal against her ear.

"Do you always do this?" he gasped suddenly.

Scarlet opened her eyes and realized that they were surrounded by flowers. Where there had been soft moss and short grass, there were now riots of knee-high flowers. Even day-bloomers were reaching for the weak moonlight, filling the entire clearing.

Scarlet laughed helplessly. "I've *never* done this," she admitted as she sat up. She held a hand to an orchid that bobbed to touch her and unfurled a happy new leaf. "It's beautiful."

"*You're* beautiful," Mal said, rising on one elbow. He traced the line of her leg with a finger that promised more of what they had just enjoyed and Scarlet had to keep herself from falling upon him once again.

"It's vanity," Scarlet confessed. "I could look my age, if I wanted. Or... if there was something you liked..." she added shyly.

Mal sat the rest of the way up. "You are perfect just this way. I want nothing else. You are exactly the Scarlet I fell in love with... the beautiful pain in my ass that told me where to shove it the very first time we talked."

Scarlet had to smile and when Mal reached to kiss her, she flowed into his arms.

When he ran out of air, she held his face in her hands for a long moment. "Did you mean it?"

"That you're beautiful?"

"That you're my... my mate." Scarlet almost didn't dare to say it.

"Can't you tell?" Mal traced the line of her neck with one finger and his breath stirred the hair that was loose around her face. "Don't you feel it?"

His touch raised fire in Scarlet's veins, but she hesitated. "If you will recall your Greek mythology, dryads are regularly described as lusty," she said primly. "I run hot, and it has been a long, long time. Maybe I'm confusing need with... with..."

"With love?" Mal asked intensely.

Scarlet took her hands back from his face and then didn't know what to do with them. "We just met," she chided.

"We've known each other for more than a year," Mal pointed out, taking one of her hands in his own and kissing it. He looked insufferably pleased with himself.

"A year that you were a complete ass to me," Scarlet pointed out.

"Did I ever actually do you wrong?" Mal still had her hand, and he turned it over to lay a second kiss on her palm.

"You tried to sell my island to horrible people. You attempted to steal my staff," Scarlet reminded him, trying to dampen the desire he was igniting. She rallied. "You wanted to have Gizelle committed to a mental institution."

"I couldn't let that poor woman stay here and be destroyed," Mal said firmly. "And I gave you as many carrots as sticks. You never admitted to your staff how much I offered to pay you if you broke the lease."

It was hard to think with her hand captured in his, with his shoulders and chest bare, with the warmth of him so close it made her skin prickle. "You could have told me the truth," she pointed out faintly.

"It didn't occur to me that I needed to," Mal said. "But I'm sorry that I didn't, if that helps."

It did, somehow. "We still have a problem," Scarlet pointed out. "I would also like to not be destroyed and you said that we were running out of time."

Mal sobered.

"So tell me how you plan to battle this creature, and how I might help."

"I'll do better," Mal said, pulling away from her seriously. "I'll show you."

Chapter 15

It was full night now and the silver moon was no longer above the clearing. But they didn't need light where Mal planned to take them.

He stepped away from Scarlet, wading through knee-deep flowers that whispered against his legs and smelled like paradise. When he had enough space, he shifted and his dragon arched his neck in pleasure at his mate's admiring eyes.

He was a large dragon, in shimmering golden earth colors muted by the darkness. In sunlight, he was like tiger's eye gemstone.

I'm an earth dragon, he told Scarlet, and he felt her delight in the brush of his mind.

You're beautiful. Her mental voice had layers that spoken voices couldn't hold: admiration, wonder, curiosity.

His dragon spread his wings and sat up to turn and share a new angle.

Don't let it go to your head, Mal snorted privately. To Scarlet, he cautioned, *I cannot go deep without risking waking the wyrm. But I can take you under.*

Under the island? Scarlet looked down curiously. *Is there a cave?*

I don't need caves, Mal scoffed. He regarded her form thoughtfully. She was standing now, her pale, lithe form dressed only in her wild hair. *Your form, it is solid?*

You tell me, Scarlet teased, brushing her hair back over her shoulder.

Certainly she had been plenty to hold onto just moments before. Mal gave a huff of a dragon laugh and vowed to do further experimentation with the solidity of her form at the first available opportunity.

He crouched. *Hold onto me and don't let go. I can take you with me, but I cannot protect you if I lose contact. It's a little like Saina's ability to allow others to breathe underwater when she's touching them, but it would be much more painful than drowning.*

Where are you taking me? Scarlet asked, walking fearlessly between his forelegs and putting her hand on one of his front feet. Mal closed his claws around her waist gently and then folded his wings around them both.

Down.

He fell forward into the earth, keeping his dive shallow and quiet. Even so, the island trembled as he passed the top levels of the dirt, sliding into the bedrock that lay below. He could feel it flow through him as he sank, carefully, not too far. He could sense the creature further down and he stayed well away, near the surface. They were near the peak of the island; hundreds of feet of rock separated them.

Scarlet was alarmed at first, then Mal felt her curiosity and wonder blossom.

It's not dark, she observed in surprise.

It's not really sight, Mal tried to explain. *Not with eyes.*

The different kinds of rock were rainbows of colors, patterns of earth energy. The soil at the top was a soup of mineral hues. The stone roots of the world stretched below them in glowing tones, and the surface of the earth was like the surface of water, reflecting back a distorted view.

The threads of rock snagged and caught on him as he swam through the slabs and they made a ringing song that wasn't really sound as they dove.

Mal moved carefully, slipping through the rock gently. Even so, the resort would be getting a good tremor; Scarlet would undoubtedly bill him for the broken glassware.

He drew them back up into the clearing and as they approached the surface, they caught a glimpse of Scarlet's roots, gleaming with life and power.

You are as beautiful from below as you are from above, Mal told her.

Her laughter was flattered.

Then, not wanting to disrupt more than he had to, or risk disturbing the wyrm's slumber, Mal reluctantly returned to the air.

The ground was still resettling as he broke the surface and Scarlet nearly lost her balance on the heaving moss as he set her down again, shifting to catch her.

He needn't have bothered; it steadied at once, but the feeling of her in his arms was intoxicating, so he didn't let go.

"Did you... like it?"

Scarlet regarded him seriously. "I can't say it was comfortable," she confessed. "But it was beautiful."

"There aren't many places I can go deep without risking innocent surface casualties," Mal said regretfully. "Only a few of the stronger seams of the earth, or land where no one lives."

"You planned to fight the wyrm like that, from inside the rock?" Scarlet didn't seem to be in a hurry to be free of his embrace, letting her hands wander up his arms to his shoulders.

"We would be evenly matched on neutral ground," Mal conceded, trying to concentrate on problems that didn't involve her clever fingers and their dearth of clothing. "And if he gains the sky, my chances of success start to plummet. I don't particularly want to give up my advantage... but that was just a skim into upper bedrock. Our battle will shake the pillars of the island itself. There may not even be an island at the end of it." He did not have to add that with no island, there would be no Scarlet.

We cannot let her be destroyed, his dragon creeled.

There's a way, Mal insisted. He didn't know what it was, yet, but he was used to solving insurmountable problems and they had time before the storms crept in.

"You don't seem all that worried," Scarlet observed skeptically.

"We've got days before the storms arrive," Mal pointed out. "And your power is not to be discounted. I cannot believe that I will not be able to figure out a way to either protect your clearing from an underground battle, or fight the creature above. I'll fix this," he said confidently. "I will protect you, and I *will* fulfill my destiny."

Scarlet shook her head at him. "I want you to try another word in that sentence."

Mal was puzzled. "Fate?" he suggested, wondering if she had a problem with the word *destiny*.

"*We*," Scarlet corrected. "*We'll* fix it, *we'll* figure it out. It's my life at risk and I have no intention of sitting aside wringing my hands while you try to save me."

Mal felt something in his chest shift unexpectedly.

He'd never had a partner. He'd always relied on his own cleverness, his dragon, and his power. He had clients, and business associates, and plenty of people who were desperate to claim him as a friend to their own advantage. But wealth and magic were better allies and he'd never acknowledged the empty place that lay like a cave in the stone of his heart, or the walls that he'd built to protect it after the last of his family had died.

Those walls had cracked at the first sight of Scarlet... or maybe even before, as he had investigated her and built an impression of who she was from her selfless actions. And now she was here, with him: his soulmate, his partner.

He traced the edge of her face in wonder. "Scarlet..."

"Mal," she said warmly, and it was a thousand times more beautiful than *Mr. Moore* had ever been. Her arms were around his neck and her slim, strong body was against his. "Did I warn you about the lusty part?" she purred, her mouth near his. "We have a few hours before I can do anything about the evacuation... and I don't need sleep."

Mal could only growl in reply and catch her in his arms and kiss her. He laid her down in the mossy flowers of the clearing and the earth rose up to meet them. They were two of a kind, isolated by their strength, sharing powers of earth. He felt like every moment of loneliness was swept away at the touch of her mouth and the stroke of her fingers.

Show her, his dragon begged. *Show her that she is our mate, that there is no room for doubt between us, that we are hers.*

Mal could feel it, that bright, unbreakable bond, streaked with need and longing and joy. "I love you," he murmured between kisses, knowing that it was pitiful compared to the strength and the beauty of what they shared. "I will love you to the end of the world and I give you everything that I am and everything I have and everything I will ever be."

She gave a small wordless keen of pleasure and surrender and Mal set himself to satisfying the needs of her nature.

Chapter 16

Scarlet met Graham at the entrance to the courtyard, her phone with the text she'd just sent in her hand. Sunrise was staining the sky.

"Graham, thank you for coming so quickly. I need an emergency staff meeting. All the senior and secondary staff, please, within the hour. We'll meet at the event hall; there isn't space for everyone in our usual room."

Graham cleared his throat. "Ah, Scarlet?" he asked, gesturing behind her.

Scarlet turned, to find that the courtyard behind her had erupted into bloom. Every plant that ever put out a flower had done so, and in many cases, glorious clusters of them. Some of the plants had changed colors, showing off their most flamboyant hues, regardless of the season.

"Oh, hmm," Scarlet said, looking over the blossom-crowded room. *Oops.*

A swollen bud gave an audible little pop as it burst into flower and a vine unfurled a whole flurry of folded up leaves and fresh buds.

"This is new," Graham observed.

Scarlet blushed.

Graham's eyes narrowed suspiciously.

"I'll keep it under control," Scarlet promised. Another flower unfolded petals and the hedge leading down into the resort was rather suddenly peppered with white blossoms.

"This have to do with Beehag's lawyer?" Graham guessed.

My mate, Scarlet thought, for a moment so giddy and full of tangled emotion that she almost forgot he had come to destroy her resort.

Graham was still looking at her dubiously and Scarlet realized that she was smiling foolishly at him. "It's complicated," she said, in vast understatement. "Please get everyone ready as quickly as you can."

After he left, Scarlet closed her eyes and tried to center herself. It felt so unreal, to feel so happy, to know that so much was at risk.

Mal seemed confident he—that *they*—could find a solution to the wyrm problem that didn't involve the destruction her tree, but she could see the fear and worry beneath that.

Together, *together,* they would be able to make it work. They were both strong and clever, and with their combined might, there must be a way to overcome the wyrm.

She went into her office to see if the printer needed more paper and to gather the rest of the notes she had taken.

First, she had to make certain that the people who trusted her with their safety were taken care of. She knew they weren't going to like what she had to tell them.

SCARLET DIDN'T HAVE to wait for the staff to grow quiet; they were already poised in anxious expectation. So many dear faces, so many people she had come to consider friends and closer.

She didn't try to soften the blow. "The island has come under an emergency storm evacuation warning. We will be closing indefinitely. We need to safely and calmly evacuate all guests and staff as quickly as possible."

There was stunned silence. Whatever they had expected, this was not it.

"I have already contacted the charter and they will be able to get a plane here three times today in total, which should be sufficient to clear out the guests and about two-thirds of the staff in coordination with using our boat to take trips to the mainland; Travis, that will be your focus today. I've started negotiations with hotels along the coast to take our clients. The restaurant will remain open with full services as long as possible, if you are willing, Chef. The spa is to be closed and all activities will be canceled. We'll leave the bar open unless it proves problematic. Tex, please use your best judgment."

She calmly called off the remainder of the assignments:

"Lydia, I'd like your staff to assist with letting the guests know about our predicament and prioritizing the ones who should be evacuated first." Lydia had a quiet manner suited to keeping people from panic and her beauty team was well-trained in deflecting drama. "I have printed out a letter of explanation to be distributed that should answer most of their questions and explain the evacuation procedure."

"Liam, I want you and the elders on the first flight out. I've got housing reserved for you in San Jose. It's just a warehouse with some bunk beds, I'm afraid. There wasn't time to find anything more suitable but I hope to have something more long term in place by the end of today so you shouldn't have to stay there long." Liam ran a modest shifter retirement home and, among other complications, needed a place where an elderly mammoth shifter with poor shifting control could have 'accidents.'

"Wrench, Graham, I'm not expecting any major trouble, but I'd like you to keep order. The perceived pinch point will be the shuttle to the airstrip, so I'd like you to maintain a presence there and respond to other incidents as needed. You'll want to keep an eye on the dock as well, keep in touch with Travis about his schedule."

She put down her clipboard. "Please pack everything you need and do not assume that return to the resort will be possible. This is not a drill. The storm shouldn't hit for several days yet, so anyone willing to stay through to tomorrow and help buckle down the resort will be very appreciated; the last group will go by boat to the mainland. There are sign up sheets by the kitchen for each of the charters."

Whispers of speculation and surprise rose as she paused. Scarlet watched some of them surreptitiously check with their smartphones, muttering about the poor data connection. They swiftly found the confirmation that Mal had promised in dire articles with splashy, threatening headlines.

She cleared her throat and they all fell silent again. "Jenny, I would like you to cancel the resort sale, return any collected funds, and sever outstanding contracts. You will each be receiving a severance package based on longevity that I hope you will find an ample cushion for this blow. Please double-check the contact address I have on file so that follow-up paperwork can be sent to you in a timely way. I have enjoyed working with every one of you and am grateful for your efforts and work ethic. That is all."

She didn't linger, but she wasn't surprised when she heard urgent footsteps behind her as she left the hall to start in on the list of guests she wanted to inform personally.

"What the hell?"

She turned to find that Graham had beat the others out. She could hear loud conversation in the event hall behind them and kept walking.

"Between the return of Alice's money and your severance pay, you should be able to retire to your own private island if you wanted to," she said conversationally. "Find a place with good soil and plant a new garden. Take some starts, if you want. We have some plants you can't find elsewhere."

Graham took her boldly by the arm. "I don't give a damn about the money," he growled, pulling her to a stop. "Or the plants. What the hell is going on with the island? What about *you*? If the storm is severe enough to evacuate the resort, what happens to your... to *you*?"

Sometimes she saw more of his grandfather in him than she should. "I will be fine," she said, resisting the urge to pat his cheek. "But I can't protect myself and everyone else who is here at the same time."

"This has everything to do with that *lawyer*," Graham snarled. "What has he done? What lies is he telling you now?"

"Mal is not our enemy," Scarlet said firmly.

"You're certainly on a first name basis now." Graham's eyes were narrow and accusatory.

Scarlet wanted to explain, badly. She wanted to tell Graham every part of it, from the heady dawning certainty that

Mal really, truly was her mate, to the danger that lurked beneath the island. "You have to trust me," she said simply. "I will tell you everything when I have a moment to breathe. But we have to get the innocent people off of this island as soon as possible, now. We don't have much time, and I need your help with that."

Graham opened his mouth to continue his protest, then snapped it shut as there was a sudden, rolling rumble and the ground beneath them gave a wild leap. Graham staggered, while Scarlet swayed in place. Someone screamed and there was the sound of shattering glass from the bar. Gravel danced at their feet and finally—after much longer than most of their usual small quakes—the earth stilled again.

Scarlet stared down, wondering if she should be concerned. Had the wyrm woken? But it was quiet now and the upheaval she was braced for never happened. She raised her gaze to Graham's concerned blue eyes. "That may make our evacuation job a little easier. Please go help Tex clean up the bar. I'm going to see Conall and work on getting Gizelle to safety."

He didn't follow her again when she resumed her swift travel across the resort.

Chapter 17

Mal picked up the masks that had fallen from the walls and straightened the artwork. The wyrm was restless, which wasn't unexpected, given the storms that were just days away. This was the light sleep before he woke, the slow stirring of a waking beast.

He had a problem in front of him.

This wasn't unusual. His entire life, both his law career and his pursuit of magic, had involved solving one problem after another, in calculated order.

Distilled to the bones, he had two choices: battle the wyrm beneath the island, or above it.

He had prepared—for decades—to fight it in his own element, deep in the earth, knowing that the resort, the compound, every living thing on the surface might be a casualty of their fight, but confident in his ability to win easily in this manner.

That was before he had realized that his mate was an irrevocable *part* of that island, and that she was, if not a certain, at least a very probable casualty of a pitched underground battle.

He only had to think of her, the flash of her hair, the silky touch of her skin, the stubborn set of her smile, to know that it wasn't a risk he was willing to take.

106

He had already all but eliminated the possibility of removing Scarlet's tree to safe location. It would require a larger portal than he had ever created and he was doubtful of the safety of transplanting a tree of that age and size even if he could manage it. Could she even leave the rest of her forest behind? He made a note to do more research and to consult with Scarlet on the topic, but he didn't consider it a likely avenue. Not in the few days that they had available.

Everything pointed to fighting the wyrm above the island.

Mal was a capable flyer and a more than competent warrior in air, just as he was in earth.

But with the wyrm in the air, came the wyrm's powers of air and water. He would be fighting in a powerful storm, at a difficult disadvantage. And he would have to win swiftly, decisively, before the storm damaged the island—and Scarlet's tree—effectively undermining his attempt to keep her safe in the first place.

He could construct a magical shield. That would protect her from flying debris and falling trees, but it wouldn't do anything to stabilize the earth beneath her. And it would be a challenge to maintain a shield larger than any he'd ever made around her while in the midst of a fight.

We have to protect her, his dragon fretted, like a dog on a bone.

There is a way, Mal insisted. *We are neglecting one thing: Scarlet herself.*

She had a sizzling power of her own. There was a way to use that, there had to be.

If he could teach her to stabilize her own piece of land, perhaps she would be able to survive the upheaval that his underground battle would cause. She was a creature of earth like he was; perhaps he could show her how to strengthen the stone beneath her.

Her magic felt raw, elemental. It wasn't anything like his ordered arsenal of spells. It wasn't shifter magic, and he didn't know if his techniques would be the slightest bit effective with her kind of power.

He rolled his shoulders back and sighed. He could almost hear his father's voice in his ear. *What's the first thing you do when you have a problem to solve?*

Mal had resented his destiny, as a boy who wanted nothing more than to be a boy. But his life had never had time for games or play.

From the time he could walk, he was learning how to control magic; his earliest runes were tattooed to his forearm when he was still barely speaking. He clearly remembered his father's arms around him. *It's good that it hurts*, he'd said, while Mal tried desperately not to cry. *Magic always has a price. Remember that.*

From the time he could shift, Mal was learning to fight, flung into hopeless battles with older, stronger dragons and shifters. He had lost repeatedly, failing over and over... until suddenly he didn't.

You don't have to be stronger than your enemy if you are smarter and faster, his father pointed out. *And there is one edge you should always have.*

Magic? eleven-year-old Mal had guessed.

Even that can be taken, his father explained patiently. *Knowledge,* knowledge *is your greatest advantage. Know your enemy, know their weaknesses, and better yet, know how to pre-*

vent having to battle them altogether. Not all fights are claws and spells.

It had taken Mal years to understand that, years alone, spent honing magic, fighting, and later learning law.

The first step was always research. *Know your enemy... and know your allies.* Mal looked at his phone and frowned at the weak WiFi signal. He stood, gameplan firmly in mind, and traced a doorway in the air ahead of him. The air sizzled, and his library opened up before him. Two more destinations, and several armfuls of books, and he settled in to learn as much about Scarlet and her curious power as possible.

A fierce knock at the door startled him. "Come!" he called.

Graham didn't look like he'd come for a social call, a scowl across his face as angry as his knock. He opened the door, then paused in the doorway, hands balling into fists at his side.

Mal was amused. "I assure you, force won't be necessary. Come in, Grant Lyons, I have questions for you."

"I'm not here to answer your questions," Graham growled as he stepped into the cottage. "I'm here to find out what you've done to Scarlet."

In a moment of pure mischief, Mal nearly told him *exactly* what he'd done to Scarlet, laying her back in the moss with her hair loose, kissing her neck, coaxing those noises of pleasure from her parted lips... he managed to keep himself from speaking, but Graham seemed to take the grin he wasn't able to smother quite personally.

"You keep your hands off of her and your nose out of her business," Graham snarled. "I don't know what you've said to her, but you can't stop the sale of the resort and this evacuation is *bullshit.*"

Mal sobered. "I assure you, it isn't."

Graham closed the distance between them. "This is Scarlet's resort. You can't take it from her without going through *me*."

We can go through him easily, Mal's dragon hissed, suggesting that they do exactly that.

But Mal restrained himself from rising to the gardener's threat, choosing instead to sit and gesture Graham to a free chair. Graham crossed his arms over his chest and remained standing. "Suit yourself," Mal said mildly. "Can you tell me what her powers entail? That pressure in the room when she's angry, do you know how she causes that? I presume it's an instinctive power; she doesn't have any of the usual trappings of structured magic."

Graham's expression of confusion and mistrust only deepened. "I'm not telling you *anything*," he said shortly.

Mal sighed. "I understand that you have no reason to believe me, but I am actually pursuing Scarlet's best interests here."

Graham snorted, but his initial bluster had muted as Mal continued to maintain his composure, to his dragon's disappointment.

"A terrible battle is coming to this island," Mal said frankly. "And the more I know about Scarlet, the better I'll be able to protect her." He gestured to the books: a selection of mythology and magic.

"Scarlet doesn't need protecting," Graham growled. "What kind of battle?" he added.

"The kind of battle that isn't yours to fight," Mal said cuttingly. "This is my fight, and I'm sorry that it had to happen here of all places, but I don't have the time or energy to watch over a bunch of misfit shifters who aren't smart enough to get out of the way. My first goal is making sure that my mate and I get out of this alive and if you aren't going to be helpful to *me*, I suggest that you go help Scarlet with the evacuation."

Graham's whole body changed, reflecting his astonishment. "Your *mate*?"

"Scarlet is my mate," Mal said. It was an unexpected new thrill to say it out loud, even if the audience was looking more distrustful than impressed.

"If you're pretending... if this is some kind of game..."

Mal flowed to his feet. "I don't have time to convince you and I don't care if you believe me." He was as tall as Graham and as powerfully built. "All you need to know is that I will do everything I can to save her."

Graham looked back at him with challenge and didn't say anything, clearly not convinced... and not ready to back off. They stared at each other for a long, silent moment.

"I don't trust you," Graham said frankly. "You act like you're better than everyone, like you know more, like that gives you the right to make decisions for the rest of us. I don't know what you're trying to do here, but if you hurt Scarlet, you'll be sorry you ever set foot here."

"I have no desire to hurt Scarlet. I want to save her."

"Do you love her?"

The question stole Mal's breath. "More than I ever thought possible," he admitted.

"Then why are you making her give up everything she's worked so hard for?" Graham demanded.

"I'm not," Mal said as calmly as he could manage. "It's complicated. There's a fight coming—"

"We'd fight for *Scarlet*," Graham growled, his emphasis implying that he'd rather leave Mal to defend himself.

"This isn't a fight for fists," Mal said impatiently. "This is a fight far beyond anything you could possibly imagine and you'd only be in the way."

Graham took that about as well as Mal expected him to, turning red and growling before he turned and stomped away.

Chapter 18

Conall's cottage had been fitted with a visual door alert; when Scarlet pushed the doorbell, the lights inside flashed so that Conall would know someone was there even if he didn't have the assistance of Gizelle's touch.

"Come!" he called gruffly.

Several items of artwork had fallen off of the wall in the rumbling earthquake, and one of the kitchen table chairs was on its side.

Gizelle was at one end of the couch, curled into a tight shivering ball and Conall was standing beside her. "She's doesn't like the earthquakes," he said to Scarlet. "And that was one of the worst yet."

Scarlet took a gentle seat next to her but didn't touch her. "Gizelle, I've come to talk about going away." Though her words were pitched for the young woman, she was carefully facing Conall.

Conall scowled at her, glancing at Gizelle. Her face was still buried in her knees, her hair tangled loose around her, and she was trembling violently. "What's this about?" he hissed. "Who's going away?"

"You two," Scarlet said serenely. "We're evacuating the resort..."

Conall's face grew alarmed. "You can't just spring this on us," he growled angrily. "What's happening? Is it the earthquakes?"

For a moment, Scarlet thought she would tell him the same story that she was giving the guests, that there was a terrible storm coming, that it wouldn't be safe for anyone on the island... it was the truth and she could keep the details vague.

Instead, she bowed her head and touched Gizelle gently on the shoulder. The young woman startled, but didn't pull away. Scarlet thought her shivering was a little less.

"There is a battle coming," she said carefully, looking up at Conall. "A battle that may not leave the resort in one piece. This earthquake was just a hint of what's to come."

Conall stared at her. "A battle that *what*? With *who*?"

Scarlet chuckled humorlessly. "An ancient two-headed monster who has been asleep beneath the island for hundreds of years."

Conall squinted at her mouth dubiously. "A what?"

"An ancient two-headed wyrm," Scarlet said, then shook her head. That might be nonsense if Conall didn't have context. What could she say that be easy to lipread?

Conall put his hand tentatively on Gizelle and flinched at the contact.

"A great, feathered, two-headed wyrm that has been imprisoned underneath the island, hellbent on the destruction of the world."

"Feathers..." Gizelle moaned. "Rain and wind. I don't want to, don't make me..."

"No one is going to make you do *anything*," Conall said fiercely, glaring at Scarlet. "I'm going to need a hell of a lot more information than that."

"We're evacuating the resort today, but there will be a few days before the danger is imminent," Scarlet said as calmly as she could. Gizelle leaned into Conall's hand, and he rubbed her cheek with his thumb. His touch had calmed her, but she was still shivering. "We can arrange private transport for you, of course. I presume you'll want to take her to Boston, and if you want to talk about sedation..."

"No, no sedation," Conall said firmly. "I'll handle the details." He seemed inclined to believe her, at least.

"I'm canceling the lease, of course, and the purchase of the island altogether. I'm having Jenny see what I need to do to return everyone's payments."

"You're treating this as a pretty final thing," Conall observed.

Scarlet met his eyes without flinching. "I don't want any loose ends in case I'm not around to tie them up later."

Conall's nostrils flared in alarm and his eyebrows knit. "Is that likely?"

Scarlet didn't have an answer for him. Mal seemed confident that he could find a way to protect her, but she could feel his underlying thread of doubt and worry.

"I'm not going," Gizelle said quietly. "The end was *here*." Then she lifted her head. "Is Chef still making cherry chocolate cake tonight?"

"To the best of my knowledge, yes," Scarlet said, glad to see Gizelle perk up. It wasn't often that Conall's touch couldn't calm her.

"I should wear red." The young woman slipped off the couch and padded across the cottage towards the bedroom. "So that I match the rain."

"I'll let you know what I arrange," Conall said quietly, watching her go. "I'll probably have a private jet come tomorrow afternoon."

"Conall," Scarlet said, and she wondered if he would be able to tell that her voice had cracked. "I have a favor to ask."

Conall frowned at her. "Anything," he said, his tone at cautious odds with his statement.

Scarlet had not expected it to be so difficult to make the request. "Will you take Tyrant with you?" She hastily added, "She should be with her sister, they grew up together, it's not safe here and I don't want her to get hurt..."

Conall, to Scarlet's astonishment, stepped gently forward, took her by the shoulders, and gave her one swift, utterly unexpected hug before stepping back again. "I will do anything I can to help," he said, voice clipped with embarrassment. "Anything you need." He didn't have the luxury of looking away, but he did look rather fixedly at her mouth rather than her eyes.

"Keep Gizelle safe," Scarlet said quietly. "Gizelle and Tyrant."

"You have my word," Conall promised.

Scarlet left, feeling relieved, and stepped out into an ants' nest of angry guests and flabbergasted staff members, all of whom needed reassurance and explanations that she couldn't give them. The earthquake, at least, seemed to be an extra bit of motivation to convince them that leaving really was in their best interests.

Chapter 19

M al felt Scarlet behind the door as she raised her hand to knock. He opened it with a spell as he rose to his feet and met her with a hungry kiss.

"How's the evacuation going?" Mal asked, when he had his lips back.

"As smoothly as possible," Scarlet said with great serenity, straightening her skirt as if she had not just made love to his face. "I think the timing of the earthquake was actually excellent, since it frightened a lot of people. The first flight has come and gone. Liam's elders are safely off, and the most problematic of the guests."

"Mr. scarier-than-a-dragon fire ant shifter?" Mal suggested wryly.

Scarlet rolled her eyes. "Demanded to be on the very first flight out," she scoffed. "Wanted a full refund of his expenses."

She looked around, puzzled. "You did not come with this much luggage," she said, observing the piles of books that Mal was cross-referencing.

"Portals," Mal said dismissively. "This stack is from a library in London, these are from my personal collection."

"Portals?" Scarlet looked at him in surprise. "You can do that?"

Mal took no small amount of pleasure in being able to impress her. "It's fairly straightforward, if I've been somewhere before," he said with a modest shrug. "The power required depends on the distance." He wouldn't need to start conserving energy for a few more days.

Scarlet gave him a narrow-eyed look. "That... would be very convenient. Guests would pay a great deal to bypass the hassle of traveling by airline and it would solve probably half of our new-guest complaints. Something about crowding people into tin rockets for several hours makes everyone very grouchy." She looked excited about the idea. "Everyone says traveling would be more fun without that traveling part... could you teach *me* to do that?"

Mal smiled at her. Even now she was finding clever ways to improve her business.

They both sobered at the same moment, remembering the impending ruin of that business.

"I don't know about your capitalistic goals for it," Mal said carefully. "But I would like to do a little experimentation with your magic. I hesitate to try moving your tree, and that would take a larger portal than I've ever even heard of anyone making... but I think I can show you how to harden the earth beneath you, so that it doesn't move when I battle the wyrm below the surface. You're undeniably powerful, and you are a creature of earth like I am, so it should be simple for you to learn.

Scarlet gave him a quick glance, then looked down at the clipboard she was holding, the paper thick with notes. "We have about an hour before the next charter gets in for the next wave of evacuations. My people have things well in hand, for now." She put down the clipboard and spread her hands. "Where do we start?"

Mal began by trying to get her to transform dirt to sturdy stone.

"How?" Scarlet asked.

Mal turned his forearms, showing her the runes. "Each of these has meaning, and a spoken word that accompanies it. Corbin's acolytes—" he snarled the name "—only memorized chants and never understood a word of them, but there are layers of meaning, and a decent warlock can modify a spell on the fly, simply by changing the order of the runes." He touched the symbols one by one. "Sleep, *nurl*. Help, *ashenad*. Build, *yawen*. Hinder, break, go, see..."

Scarlet touched one of them curiously and Mal had to tamp down the desire that even a casual a touch caused. "This one is on Breck's wrist, from the engagement bracelet he shares with Darla."

"Join, *sheln*," Mal said and he said it more intensely than he intended. Scarlet eyes were hot and mirrored his own need. It would be entirely too easy to get distracted.

But as much as he wanted to lay her down and kiss her into filling the room with flowers, he needed to save her much more. "I made those bracelets with the purpose of helping soulmates find each other, at the request of Darla's father, who very much hoped that she would find true love."

Scarlet's needy look turned instantly to irritation. "Do I have you to thank for that nightmare of a wedding, as well?" she asked in exasperation.

Mal grimaced. "I'm afraid so, at least in some small part. Though I am sure that Darla's *charming* mother would have found something else to sue over even if everything else had gone to plan. You do not need to worry about the lawsuit," he was quick to assure her. "The case will be settled quietly out of court. My treat."

Scarlet didn't look terribly mollified. She only frowned and touched one of the runes he had already pointed out. "*Ashenad*," she said firmly, and she held out her opposite arm.

A gleaming rune, a perfect duplicate of Mal's, appeared on both her arms.

He scowled to cover his surprise as she turned her arms to inspect her work. "It's meant to be a painful ordeal. You have to suffer for every rune and gain understanding through trial."

Scarlet raised an eyebrow at him. "*Yawen*," she said, and a second shimmering rune appeared at her wrist. "Is there one for protect?"

Mal showed it to her and told her the word. "You're *supposed* to spend a week or more meditating over the order for your rune tattoos, because they will define you as a warlock forever." He sounded sulky to his own ears.

"Do we *have* a week for meditation?" Scarlet asked scathingly as a third rune appeared on her fair skin.

"Probably not," Mal admitted.

"I can rearrange them anyway," Scarlet said, demonstrating by switching two of them and Mal couldn't quite keep from sputtering in protest. "Is there a rune for turn-dirt-into-stone?"

"There is no single rune for that. You would build that out of words, like writing a sentence."

"What other runes will I need to do this, then?"

Mal shook his head in wonder. "This one," he said, rolling his arm over. "It translates as roots, though it can also mean ancestors. I think that's particularly appropriate for you."

They added protect, *djek*, and strength, *rawen*.

And at the very end, she whispered, "*Sheln*," and when the join rune was on her skin, completing a circlet of her wrist, Mal felt a jolt of power settling into place.

This could work, he thought, full of optimism.

Chapter 20

I t didn't work.

Scarlet spoke the runes perfectly, touching each one, and... nothing happened.

"Is it because I'm touching them?" she asked, disappointed. "You just gesture a bit, should I also?"

"That usually comes with practice," Mal explained. "I don't have to touch them to activate them anymore, but I did when I was first learning."

Mal walked through a simple shield spell that he'd started with as a young man and brought a flaring egg of glittering power around him to life. Scarlet tossed a pen at him curiously and it snapped and fell, charred, to the ground without touching him.

Scarlet rearranged her runes, followed his steps, and mimicked his chant, with and without touching the runes directly... and still nothing happened. She couldn't alter dirt, or move it at all, and she couldn't bring up a simple shield.

Mal sighed in frustration. "I can feel the power," he said, peering at her inert runes and stroking them with his thumbs, agitated. They were sitting together on his porch; they'd already set off the fire alarm once experimenting with Mal's shields. "I can sense it. You're saying the words correctly, I can even feel your will. By rights, this ought to work."

"Who taught you?" Scarlet asked, putting her free hand on his shoulder. "How old were you?"

Mal's strokes on her skin slowed. "My father taught me, when I was very young. He knew that I would be the next in line to battle the wyrm, and I spent my childhood learning to tap into my shifter power and fight."

"You were close with your father," Scarlet guessed.

Mal's head bowed. "Yes," he said simply. Scarlet gave him space and after a moment he went on. "I was a mage before I was a man, and I lost him shortly after that," he said grimly, standing and walking to the porch railing. "But he taught me everything he... thought I needed to know. He was a brilliant teacher."

"Don't think for a moment that you aren't, just because I can't seem to wield power the way you do," Scarlet said, aching to see him doubting himself.

Scarlet looked at the silhouette of him, gloomy against the brilliant sunset sky. When she'd imagined Mr. Moore, the lawyer, she'd pictured him as a shallow old man, set in his ways and stubborn, not willing to take her seriously as a woman.

Instead, he'd proved to be complicated, appealingly *good*, and dazzling handsome, with just a trace of silver in his hair to hint at his wisdom. And he listened to her, his brown eyes unexpectedly gentle, his hands warm and strong, his skin...

Scarlet shook her head and reminded herself to focus.

"Mal..." The idea had come to her some time earlier, but it was a wild gamble, a terrible risk.

"I've been looking at shield spells," he said, voice determined. "Something I could set beforehand and don't have to feed with magic while I'm fighting. I've done hoard locks before, and they're complicated, they require a lot of setup. We still have a few days, so I could probably work something out."

If she was wrong about him... If she was only blinded by her attraction, fooled by his flattery...

"Mal," she repeated more firmly.

"I could solidify the earth below your tree myself, I think, too," Mal said, thumbing absently through the book in his hand. "Make a safe place that wouldn't be damaged. But it would take months to do it so that I don't have to hold it together while I fight, and we have days, not months." He had clearly hoped that she would be able to hold the spell herself and Scarlet felt guilty that she couldn't manage something so simple.

She closed the distance between them and put her hands on his broad back, letting her head lean between his shoulders. "You could bind me."

Mal went rigid. "Scarlet..." He shrugged from her embrace and turned to face her, shaking his head.

"I know what I'm asking."

"You have no *idea* what you're asking."

"I'm asking you to save me," Scarlet reminded him. "I have a certain amount at stake here, too."

Mal's mouth worked silently a moment and he stalked away, to the end of his porch. The book was tossed carelessly to his table. "What Corbin and his acolytes did, that was unconscionable. I couldn't do that."

Scarlet followed him. "But if you had my power at your command, you could meet the wyrm in his own domain, battle and defeat him."

"At what cost?" Mal asked the porch railing tightly. "You'd lose yourself."

"It wouldn't be like that," Scarlet reminded him. "I would be *willing*."

"You might go into it thinking you were," Mal said, turning to face her. "But that spell, that spell was made to control, to sap will and drain humanity. It wasn't designed to let you retain your own self-awareness."

"I'm not a shifter," Scarlet pointed out. "There's no reason to think it would affect me the same way."

"It's not worth the risk," Mal said ferociously.

"It's my risk to take," she answered just as fiercely.

Mal gazed at her stubbornly and she glared back.

The cautious part of her wanted to claim that what she felt for him was mere attraction, a simple physical reaction to a smart, sexy man who checked off all her feature requests and had hands that could make her body sing.

But it wasn't her body that was singing, she was reluctant to admit.

It was her soul.

Deep within her own chest, she could feel the mate-bond, like a shy bird fluttering in the cage of her ribs.

Mal, for all of his arrogance and irritating confidence, for every one of his flaws, was a kindred spirit. He was lonely beneath his beautiful veneer, isolated by power and position, and his heart was filled with a yearning so familiar that Scarlet could barely tell where her desire ended and where his began.

"Scarlet..."

"You *are* my mate," she said, savoring the words as she faced them at last. "And I am already bound to you."

Saying it aloud unleashed every last reservation. Scarlet closed her eyes and brought her hand to his chest, letting her power flow into him.

Mal made a strangled noise. She found her center and pulled back. "Did I hurt you?" she asked anxiously, but she knew she hadn't.

He stared at her in wonder.

"You are more than I ever imagined..." he breathed. "I cannot fail—"

He stopped himself, then stepped closer. "*We* cannot fail," he corrected himself, and when he brought his mouth to Scarlet's, every tree within a hundred feet burst into bloom.

Chapter 21

Mal would have liked to spend more time experimenting with Scarlet's power... or exploring her kisses with the new strength of their mate-bond.

But time was one thing they didn't have.

She drew back reluctantly. "I have to go. There are angry guests gathering, and I can't leave Graham and Wrench to deal with them alone."

"Do you always know what is going on, everywhere at the resort?" Mal had to ask.

Scarlet, leaving one last kiss along his jaw that he knew was going to burn for hours after she left, shook her head. "Not always, everywhere. I have to think about someone to know where they are, or think about a place and know what is happening there."

She closed her eyes and showed him, and it was a weird and dissociated feeling, like he was looking down at the courtyard by her office using some kind of heat vision. Someone was snapping with anger and fear, another was a tangle of anxiousness, another frustrated and confused. What he saw was much more about what they were feeling than what they looked like.

"I have to go," she said apologetically. Before he could ask when she would be back, or any of the hundreds of questions that were crowding his mind, she vanished from his arms.

Mal wondered if he'd ever get used to the sense of loss when she did that, but was comforted by the feel of her inside his chest. He would never lose her, they would never truly be apart.

Our mate, his dragon sighed happily. *Forever.*

He looked at the book he had tossed on the table and narrowed his eyes thoughtfully. Trying to very specifically draw only on the power through the gleaming mate-bond inside, he muttered a short spell and gestured.

The book shot open, flipped through every page like a crazed fan, and violently shut again, nearly bouncing off the table.

What are you doing? Scarlet demanded in his head.

Sorry, Mal laughed helplessly. *I was experimenting, did I bother you?*

I'm trying to evacuate my resort and that's very distracting, Scarlet said impatiently. Then she softened. *It tickles.*

I'll keep it to a minimum, Mal promised.

She gave him a parting caress of her mind, like a kiss on the cheek, and Mal refrained from disturbing the mate-bond again.

He cleaned up the books he'd brought in, returning the stacks to the library through a portal that he had to consciously not draw from Scarlet's abundant energy. If the library was alarmed by the swift return, they were professional enough not to comment by his unexpected arrival.

As full as he was, with her bright power, and the warm presence of her, Mal became aware that his body was hungry. He considered using a portal to obtain a meal, but steeled himself to have dinner at the restaurant instead. He was, after all, pay-ing a considerable amount for gourmet food, and whatever else he was, he was not too cowardly to face Scarlet's staff again.

The glow of Scarlet's mate-bond also helped him admit to himself that he also wanted the companionship of the restaurant. He was tired of solitary meals and isolated studies.

Breck gave him a curious look when he arrived at the restaurant, but led him to a table without comment. It was the same table that Mal had seated himself in the morning before, and he guessed that wasn't a coincidence.

Breck poured him a tall glass of cold water. "Our dinner menu tonight is your choice of a halibut with cream sauce and dill, served with either a baked or mashed potato side, or a Mediterranean lamb roast with young root vegetables and a reduced olive glaze."

"Lamb," Mal selected mildly, and both of them pretended that there was not any more important conversation they could possibly have than the choice of drink to accompany it, even though Breck was clearly dying for more information.

It was quiet; most of the guests had already been evacuated, and several members of the staff were murmuring and watching him not at all surreptitiously as they helped themselves from the buffet.

Mal was not unaware of the entrance of Alice, Amber, and Mary, but he was surprised when Alice led them in a beeline directly to his table.

"Mind if we sit with you?"

Alice, her head cocked in challenge, towered over Mal where he was seated. Mary and Amber looked dubious, but when Mal graciously gestured at the empty chairs, they all took seats. Alice was brave enough to sit beside him, while Mary timidly took the seat across from him and Amber awkwardly lowered herself into the remaining chair.

Breck returned to pour everyone water and give the dinner choices, a distinct lack of flirtation in his service.

"I am surprised to see you two here still," Mal observed across the table, once the waiter had returned to the kitchen with their choices.

Alice snorted. "Neither Neal nor Tony are particularly happy with it," she observed frankly. "But you try telling Amber to do anything. She looks all sweet and pliable, but good luck getting her to comply."

Amber looked abashed by the honest assessment and Alice cleared her throat. "I mean... you're leaving on the boat first thing tomorrow morning, right Amber?"

"Yes," Amber said shortly, taking a sip of her water.

Mal, following Alice's blunt example, gathered himself. "Amber, I'd like a moment to speak with you alone, if you're willing."

Amber stared at him with alarmed golden eyes.

Mary squirmed. "We could get salads from the buffet..." she started to suggest politely.

"No," Alice said flatly. "Look, no one knows what you're up to here, or what you've done to Scarlet, but I'm not real excited to leave my pregnant friend in your clutches for a conversation."

Mal protested, "I assure you—"

"Your *pregnant* friend?" Amber exclaimed in disgust. "*Really*, Alice?"

Alice still had her baleful gaze fixed on Mal. "I promised Tony I wouldn't let you out of my sight for a second."

"I think you could see anything that was going to go wrong from across the restaurant full of shifters," Amber pointed out.

"I want to be in hitting distance," Alice declared.

"I wish I were in hitting distance," Amber muttered, glaring across the table at her.

Mary looked like she wanted to fold into her chair and die.

"It can wait," Mal said peacefully.

Amber gave him a piercing look. "You can say anything you have to say to me in front of them," she said firmly.

"I was sorry to miss your mother's visit," Mal said gently. "I would have preferred to tell her what I found out about your father in person."

Everyone at the table stiffened and Mal steeled himself.

"My... father?" Amber said numbly, with a hand to her belly.

"If you'd prefer to..."

"What do you know about my father?" Amber demanded, bringing a fist down on the table that made all the glasses jump.

Mal kept his voice low. "You're aware of the warlock Corbin and his... use of shifters."

Amber's face went white.

"Your father's sole goal was to keep you from Corbin's clutches," Mal said gently. "I don't believe he would have given you up for any other reason. My guess is that he knew he was close to capture."

Amber was staring down at the surface of the table, taking careful breaths. Alice swore quietly. Mal was surprised by his own sympathy. He usually maintained a professional detachment from this sort of thing, but the look on Amber's face cut deeper than it should.

"I've... there's a fund set up for victims of the warlock and his—"

Amber surged to her feet, shoving her chair back hard. "Maybe it's hard for you to understand, but money doesn't *fix* everything," she snarled at him.

Mal took her outburst without comment. "I'm sorry for your—"

"I'm not hungry," Amber growled and she stormed as gracefully as she possibly could for the entrance to the restaurant.

Alice rose to follow her, shooting Mal a baleful look over her shoulder as she called to Amber to wait for her.

Mary remained behind. Her look was thoughtful and measuring. Mal remembered that she was the timid one of the bunch and was surprised that she didn't flee at the first opportunity.

Instead, they sat for a long moment in silence, regarding each other.

"Are you the one who set up the anonymous trust for the victims of Beehag's zoo?" she finally asked.

"Yes," Mal said simply.

"You did that for Benedict Beehag, as his lawyer, because of the horrible things that his uncle had done?"

"No," Mal said shortly. He had tried to convince Benedict to set something up, but the heir to the Beehag fortune had proved to be as self-centered and shallow as Mal had come to expect of billionaires; even the promise of a tax shelter had not strong-armed generosity from him.

"You made secrecy about the payment a condition of the allotment," Mary observed. "Neal almost didn't take it."

"I'm glad he did," Mal said.

"I'm trying to decide if I should thank you," Mary said honestly. "On the one hand, that money made it much easier for him to change careers and get his life back. On the other... it feels like dirty money."

Mal was having to reconsider Mary; though she was quiet and unsure compared to the forward, forthright Alice, the deer shifter was no coward. He sighed. "Because I've been trying to get Scarlet to sell out her lease?"

"She loves the resort. This is her home. Why would you try to take that from her? I take a dim view of anyone who can't take no for an answer."

Mal wasn't used to justifying himself to anyone, let alone *wanting* to. He made the best choices with the information he had, and he almost always had *more* information than anyone. He never felt the need to waste time seeking approval for the choices he made, and his ego didn't need stroking.

But he found himself wanting to explain himself to Mary... to the entire staff of Shifting Sands and all the people who cared for Scarlet.

"I'm willing to admit I made a mistake with Scarlet," he said honestly. "I made assumptions I should not have." He did not add that it was a very reasonable expectation that Scarlet could have rebuilt elsewhere. It had never even occurred to him that she would be literally incapable of leaving the island.

He wondered what other assumptions would prove false.

"I have the lamb for the lawyer," Breck said, clearing his throat. He looked askance at the chairs Alice and Amber had vacated; their meals were balanced on his tray. "And halibut for the *deer* Mary?" He paused a moment before putting Mary's down, giving her a chance to declare her intention to switch seats.

But Mary only smiled. "Thank you, Breck."

The waiter spread a napkin into her lap as Mal laid out his own.

The food—hot and fresh this time—was everything that he had hoped for, with balanced spice and perfectly cooked vegetables.

They ate quietly for a while after Breck refilled their water and left, with minimal conversation about the food. Then Mary abruptly asked, "Is it true you're Scarlet's mate?"

Mal wasn't the slightest bit surprised that she had already heard; Alice was Graham's mate, and Alice was Mary's closest friend. Honestly, Mal would not have been surprised if the entire resort knew.

"I am," he said simply.

"And you're a warlock like Corbin?"

Any warm, companionable feelings that had started to bloom in Mal's chest turned to ash. "I am *nothing* like Corbin," he said fiercely.

Mary gave his forearm tattoos a long measured look.

For a second time, Mal desperately wanted to explain, to make her hear his side of the story. "I'm not like Corbin," he reasserted. "I'm..." He paused.

"A good guy?" Mary guessed.

Mal met her gaze appraisingly. "I was going to say that I was trying to save the world, not rule it."

"Noble goal," Mary said, mopping up a last of her sauce with a piece of bread. "But goals don't define someone, their actions do."

Mal gravely replied, "Then I hope that my actions prove to you my sincerity." And he meant it with his whole heart.

Chapter 22

Scarlet hesitated on Mal's front step, her hand lifted to knock. Should she just go in? Should she simply materialize inside? She didn't know the rules of engagement for having a mate.

Just as she decided to knock, the door opened and she sucked in a breath. Mal was wearing pants, and nothing else, the broad expanse of his chest like a landscape of toned muscle.

"I wasn't sure if you needed to sleep," she said apologetically, lowering her hand.

Mal was gazing back at her. "You are so beautiful," he said in awe. "I keep thinking I've imagined you more gorgeous in my mind than you could possibly be, and then I see you again and you are so much *more*."

Scarlet hadn't thought a compliment could undo her so completely. She felt her cheeks heat and felt like a trembling sapling all over again. "I... I..." His bare chest didn't do much to help her keep her thoughts together.

Then he closed the distance between them and Scarlet was eagerly meeting him.

To her shock, he lifted her up into his arms, kissing her as he carried her into his cottage. She felt his hand make a gesture behind her and the door swung shut behind them. No one had ever carried her anywhere, and Scarlet savored the unexpected delight of it, wrapping her legs eagerly around him.

He laughed against her lips. "You weren't kidding about that whole *lusty* business, were you?"

"Let's find out together," Scarlet suggested, moving to nibble his ear.

Mal's arms tightened and he hissed in pleasure as he navigated them to his bedroom and laid her down on the broad bed. A stack of books was swept carelessly to the floor to clear space for them.

It was like being offered a buffet with too many delicious options: she wanted to kiss his amazing lips, and she wanted to spread her hands over his strong shoulders, and she wanted to wrap herself around him, and she wanted to run her fingers through his silver-touched hair, all at the same time.

And most of all, she wanted him in her, filling her physically as well as emotionally. She craved his warmth inside of her, his skin against hers, his weight... she was whimpering, tugging at the closure of his pants.

But he pressed her down onto the bed with gentle, slow kisses, thwarting her desperate efforts. "Shhh," he said, putting first one of her hands, then the other, above her head. "Shhh," he repeated, kissing sweetly down her neck.

Scarlet squirmed, but left her hands above her head obediently as he reached for the buttons of her blouse.

He unbuttoned her so slowly that Scarlet had to force herself not to hasten the process by simply unmaking her clothing out of impatience. His hands caressed everything he uncovered, in slow, unhurried worship. He followed his fingers with kisses and nibbles as he finished with the buttons and pulled her into a seated position so he could slip the blouse off her arms.

They kissed there a long moment and Mal unclasped the bra and slid the straps from her shoulders. Scarlet could not help gasping as he cupped her breasts in his hands, growling against her lips.

"Mal," she begged, clawing at his gorgeous shoulders. "Mal..." He was still wearing pants, and Scarlet was beginning to think this was a desperate injustice.

"Shhh..." he said again, leaving a trail of butterfly kisses across her cheek. Then he was pressing her back down into the bed and kissing down her belly to unzip her skirt. Scarlet lifted her hips to let him slide it down off of her, hopeful, longing, waiting for the sound of his zipper, and she was disappointed when he threw aside her skirt but returned to the bed still clothed.

Then his mouth met her nethers and Scarlet gave a cry of surprised pleasure as she took double-handfuls of the quilt beneath her. His tongue teased her, licking and probing gently, slowly, drawing out the orgasm that washed over her.

When she could see again, Mal was once again straddling her and she could feel how hard he was through his now-hated pants. "Mal..." she begged. "Mal..."

He bent to kiss her, and she tasted herself, tangy and salty, on his lips. She wrapped one leg around him and pushed him over on his back, rolling over to straddle him confidently.

"Scarlet," he started to say.

"Shhh..." she told him with a smile. Then she kissed the base of his throat, drawing a groan from his lips as he tipped his head back.

She kissed slowly down his chest, then unbuttoned his pants with her teeth, nibbling at the muscles that tensed in his stomach as she used her fingers to unzip him at last.

He sprang into her hand as she wrestled the pants down around his hips and she teased him and bent to kiss him, to draw him into her mouth as slowly as she could manage. His hips squirmed as she licked and sucked and her own desire was mounting to a new pitch as he growled her name.

When he was reduced to fragments of sentences—*please, you have to, Scarlet, wait!*—she crawled up his intoxicating body and lowered herself onto him in one smooth motion that made them both cry out. The orgasm was only the first of several, as Mal managed to hold off his own pleasure by sheer force of will and bring her again and again to climax. Scarlet wondered if he was using a spell to prolong things, he was so keyed up, and then decided to stop overthinking it and let herself enjoy the pulsing waves of bliss that he woke in her body.

At last, he joined her in one final release, desperately holding her hips as he thrust into her. Still coupled, Scarlet sank down and they lay together as their bodies shivered off the last spasms of their lovemaking.

"Scarlet," Mal said breathlessly, leaving little kisses on her forehead. "My mate."

"I... love you," Scarlet confessed.

Mal's entire body stiffened and Scarlet wondered if she'd said the wrong thing. Was it tainted by the overwhelming rush from such incredible sex? Should she have waited for the afterglow to pass?

But it wasn't the sex that made her say it; her body was already humming comfortably, but there was new need beneath it. She loved the sex, but this was more. This was his arms around her, his gentle mouth on her brow. It was the way she wanted to tell him everything and discover everything about him. It was the way she way dying to find out what his favorite food was and feed it to him, figure out where he was ticklish, learn all his habits and quirks and shyly show him hers.

It was the way she recognized herself in his eyes: all the isolation and buried desire for connection.

He made a noise that Scarlet couldn't interpret and drew her closer. "I love you," he replied, and Scarlet hadn't known that the feelings inside her could swell further.

They continued to lazily touch and caress for what might have been moments or hours, unwilling to move apart.

"You never did answer the question about whether or not you needed sleep," Scarlet reminded him, when he bent to draw the displaced quilt over them against the late night chill. He had fascinating goosebumps all along his arm. She stroked them as he folded her back into his arms.

"I have a better idea," he said, and Scarlet was delighted to feel him stir in interest against her leg.

Chapter 23

Mal fell into inevitable sleep after a second round with the fiery, insatiable dryad.

No, not insatiable, he thought, laying in his bed as he woke. He could bring her to pleasure and leave her flatteringly limp with contentment. Just... how had she put it? She ran *hot*. Every time he touched her, she was instantly interested, responsive to his touch. He smiled, still not ready to open his eyes.

Scarlet wasn't in bed with him, wasn't in his cottage at all. She was in her office, he knew, by the singing mate-bond in his heart, and when he *reached*, she answered.

You dreamed, she observed.

Of you? Mal didn't remember his dreams often.

Of deep places, Scarlet told him. She was distracted.

What are you doing?

Paperwork, Scarlet said wryly. *It's incredible how much paperwork is involved in the end of the world. I'll need your buyout offer in writing before Jenny and Travis leave. They're taking the boat to the mainland with the last of the staff once the private jet has left with Conall and Gizelle.*

All business. Focused. Mal was still half-asleep, and he tried to figure out why she felt a little different than usual, why things felt a little off. He dismissed the niggling worry as lingering concern about the looming battle.

We are ready, his dragon said confidently. *It is a good plan, and we are strong together.*

They had a few days left to perfect their synchronicity, but Mal already knew that with Scarlet's power behind his magic, there was little chance of failure. His fate felt like it was easily in hand.

Also, he was hungry.

We worked up an appetite, his dragon said smugly.

Mal threw off the sheet he'd slept under, pausing to press his face into a tangle of it and inhale Scarlet's intoxicating scent of earth and growing things.

Our mate, he thought with triumph.

He had to drag himself out of the bed with effort and after a quick shower, he dressed and decided to get a quick snack from the bar cooler.

The resort was weirdly quiet.

All the usual birds and insects were chirping, but there was no one splashing in the pool, no loud chatter at the bar, no music anywhere. The restaurant and kitchen were still; Mal had not realized what a constant Chef's singing was until it was gone.

The last of the staff would be packing, he realized with a pang. This was the end. They would leave on the boat and Conall and Gizelle would take a private jet away to a new life.

If—when—he and Scarlet were triumphant over the wyrm, the resort would still be battered by their battle. It would take time to get repairs facilitated.

He would build her a new resort, Mal thought. A better one, if she wanted. But would it ever be the same? Would the staff return, or would they take their severances and settle into new lives of luxury? He'd never seen such a close-knit found family, hadn't even realized it was possible. Was this really the end of it, as they scattered across the globe?

His thoughts took him into the back entrance of the bar, where he was startled to find exactly the staff he'd been pondering quietly sitting in a loose circle around a cluster of tables.

"I'm sorry," he said, realizing he was disrupting a private moment. "I can get something from the kitchen."

"I don't think so."

Graham was looming behind him.

Mal gave him an amused look. "Do you have to get to the point of fisticuffs with everyone, Grant?"

Lydia stood to pull up another chair, and she gave Graham a chiding look. "Please join us," she invited gently. "We all have a lot of questions."

The audience he faced would have intimidated greater men than Mal but he squared his shoulders and took the seat Lydia indicated.

Laura looked like she had been crying, her mouth a firm line in her face. Amber had clearly not forgiven him for the news he had delivered the night before and Tony looked like he would have gleefully crossed the table that separated them to claw his eyes out. Mary's expression was thoughtful, Alice looked like she'd just had a bad cup of coffee. Neal was frowning at Graham as he took a seat at the fringe of the group and Wrench looked like he was trying to figure out how to switch chairs with Lydia, who was patting Mal on the knee.

"This has come as quite a shock to everyone," Lydia said in a smashing understatement.

"Whatever you've done to Scarlet, we're not going to let you get away with it." That was Travis, crossing his arms and glaring at Mal suspiciously.

"Graham says there's a *battle* coming," Alice said, sitting forward to lean on the table towards him. "Did you mean a *legal* battle?"

"Was the evacuation really necessary?" Magnolia and Chef were even there, sitting close together in creaking chairs. Chef had clearly been cooking and there was a platter of miscellaneous leftovers that no one seemed to have touched.

The sound of a throat clearing drew them all up short and Scarlet was coming in through the back entrance to the bar, Jenny at her side with a pile of papers. Mal had to make himself scowl not to smile foolishly at her and it took him a moment to realize why she looked so different.

Her hair was down, loose over her shoulders and in thick waves down her back. Mal dearly wanted to bury his fingers in that mane, to kiss her neck... he wrenched himself back to the moment with effort.

To Mal she said, "They deserve to know the whole story. This was their home, too."

She walked into the bar like she owned it, which... she almost did. "I'm not enspelled," she assured the rest of them as she picked up a tray and began to gather abandoned glassware; everyone had undoubtedly been busy with the evacuation the night before. "I'm not being blackmailed, I'm not being paid off, Mal hasn't hypnotized me, and this isn't his fault. It's an unfortunate set of circumstances, and there are no fingers to be pointed."

"It's not because of the storms," Graham growled.

"No one believes that for a moment," Travis agreed.

"If there's some way we can help..." Lydia offered.

"Anything, darling," Magnolia added.

"Anything," Chef agreed firmly.

Scarlet gave a warm smile around the room and Mal half-expected flowers to start sprouting out from between the tiles. How had he ever thought of her as chilly?

"You have been good friends," Scarlet said. "Like family to me in all the *best* meanings of the word,"—Darla chuckled wryly—"and I have been touched and honored by your trust in me over the years, and your loyalty and your generosity."

Her voice became firm. "But this is not your fight. Beneath the island is a monster, a sleeping wyrm from prehistory. The storms that are coming are a sign that he is waking, and if he does, he will break free and destroy everything he can reach."

"The resort?" Tex asked.

"The resort," Mal interjected. "The island. The mainland towns. The nearby cities, the farms, every ship on the ocean. He is destructive and strong, and if I fail to cage him, I don't know who or what could stop him, but I know that the death toll would be unconscionable."

Graham gave him a suspicious look. "And you think *you* can cage him? By yourself."

"I know I can," Mal said confidentially. "This has always been my destiny: to fight him and win."

"What kind of monster is it?" Laura asked.

"How are you going to fight it?" Saina demanded.

"That's the rub," Mal explained. "The battle... there's going to be a lot of collateral damage. It could level the resort. Or even the whole island." He nodded at Bastian. "You've witnessed dragon battles. They banned them in Europe because of the damage they could cause. Now take that and amplify it by a creature ten times the size, with powers of water and wind and no care at all for bystanders. I cannot promise that anyone—or anything—on this island will be standing at the end of it."

Graham froze. "You can't do that."

"Oh," Lydia said with a sigh. "How terrible. The whole resort?"

"We could rebuild," Travis suggested. "On another island if this one was too wrecked up."

"The sale hasn't been accepted yet," Jenny said, eyeing Mal. "We've still got all that money we raised..."

"What about *Scarlet*?" Graham demanded.

"What *about* Scarlet?" Lydia asked. "She's evacuating too, aren't you, Scarlet? We're *all* leaving."

There was a moment of silence and everyone craned around to look at Scarlet where she was piling her tray full of glasses.

"I can't leave the island," Scarlet said with a wry little smile. "It's impossible for me to evacuate with you. I'm—"

A sudden keen and the sound of slapping footsteps preceded Gizelle's headlong race up the stairs and into the bar. She skidded to a barefooted stop at the edge of the tables. "Sweet One!" she said in alarm. "I can't find Sweet One! We can't leave without her! I won't go!" She rubbed her head and moaned. "I can't go. I haven't gone. *It's my fault.*"

Conall followed at a brisk pace. "The jet's coming in an hour and we can't find the kitten," he explained patiently, trying to comfort her. "Has anyone seen her? Gizelle, why are your hands dirty, sweetheart?"

Scarlet offered, "Tyrant was sleeping on my bed earlier, perhaps she's there?" She gave a curious expression of concentration which faded to confusion. "I... I can't..." She lifted the tray of glassware and abruptly dropped it. Glasses and bottles shattered around her.

"Scarlet..." Mal surged to his feet in alarm. Several of the others stood as well and there was a murmur of surprise and speculation.

"It was... *heavy*," she said in astonishment, staring down at the broken glass around her. "I can't remember the last time something was *heavy*..."

Then she raised her eyes to Mal and he watched shock and fear fill her face and felt his heart stop in his chest. "Something is wrong," she whispered. "Something is very, very wrong."

She vanished.

Gizelle gave a shriek and everyone else gasped.

"Scarlet!" Mal roared. "Graham, what's happened?"

Graham was already in motion. "Amber! Amber, I'm going to need your help! Now!"

Chaos ensued as he bolted for the tool shed behind the bar.

"What do you need Amber for?" Tony demanded protectively as Amber stood in confusion.

"What is going on?" "Where did she go?" "What is happening?" "Is it the monster?"

Gizelle sobbed, "It's my fault, it's all my fault," and Conall tried to comfort her.

Mal blistered the air and ripped a portal through to Scarlet's clearing without a second thought for protecting her secret.

A gasp went through the staff, but Mal didn't wait to watch their reactions before he was bolting through the glimmering doorway.

Mal was no expert on trees, but he could recognize a dying plant when he saw one.

Already, more than half of the flowers had fallen off, and the leaves were limp and curled, with alarming brown, burnt tips. The moss was carpeted in red petals.

Scarlet stood at the base of the tree, arms around the trunk. "No..." she moaned. "No..."

Mal went to her, but when he tried to take her into his arms, there was nothing *to* her. The sensation of her power was notably missing. "Scarlet...?"

She sank to her knees, forehead pressed against the bark, and Mal couldn't touch her to lift her up. "Scarlet!"

Red petals fell around them like rain.

"Grant Lyons, get your ass over here!" he shouted back through the portal. Half the staff had already come through, blinking around at the jungle glade in wonder and alarm.

Bastian followed him to Scarlet, threw his first aid kit down beside him and drew his fingers wonderingly through her. As they watched, she slowly vanished, writhing in pain.

"Scarlet's... a tree?" Saina was at his heels.

"A dryad..." Laura breathed.

"What's going on?"

"Oh, Scarlet..." Lydia murmured. "She's beautiful..."

Graham was finally there, Amber at his heels. He was holding a bucket of tools and Tony had a shovel that he clearly wasn't going to let his mate carry.

"What happened to her?" Mal demanded, just resisting the urge to take Graham by the throat. "What's wrong with her?"

"Graham, it's your missing shovel!" Travis called from the far side of the tree. "And an... empty bag of salt?"

Mal's mood changed from panicked to enraged. "What did you *do* to her?" he hissed at the gardener.

"I didn't do anything!" Graham snarled in return. "I should be asking what you've done. She was just *fine* until you got here."

"The tree has been salted!" Amber exclaimed. "Someone has dug up the roots and salted them! Oh, Scarlet!"

"Can you save her?" Mal raged. He didn't have a spell for this, and didn't have the tools to face a life without the woman who'd gone from a thorn in his side to the air that he breathed. "You have to. You have to save her."

"We can dig out the contaminated soil, but she's already absorbed so much of it..." Amber fingered a wilted leaf and shook her head. "I... don't know. This should have taken weeks to happen..."

"Out of my way," Mal warned. That was one thing he could do. The soil around Scarlet's tree boiled like water and rose up in a wave away from the trunk of the tree.

Not sure how far was far enough, Mal spun a second portal into existence and dumped the contaminated soil out into the ocean.

Amber stared at him in boggled astonishment. "Well, that's one way to do it," she squeaked.

"What now?" Mal snarled.

"Fresh dirt," Graham growled. "If it's not too late."

Amber added, "Water. Lots of water. Flush the poison out of her."

It was not too late. It could not be too late.

The other side of the clearing provided a clean source of earth, and everyone danced a moment as Mal moved the ground beneath their feet and tenderly filled in the holes he'd created.

Her red flowers continued to fall, carpeting the earth in crimson.

"It's like it's raining blood," Lydia murmured.

Gizelle, who had crept through the portal with Conall at her heels, gave a whimper of fear, trembling and weeping.

Mal barely noticed them, too consumed with anger and fear. He needed water, fresh water, and he was deeply alarmed to find it within easy reach above. The storms that should have been a few days away were already touching the far side of the island and it was a simple matter to pull in a cloud of rain that drenched the new soil and soaked everyone to the skin.

"You can stop!" Graham finally shouted, when the dirt around Scarlet's tree was churned to mud. "Stop!"

Mal released the tendril of cloud with effort and the rain slowed; water was not easy for him to control.

He staggered over the mud to fall at the base of Scarlet's tree. He leaned against the trunk of her tree.

"Scarlet," he begged. "Scarlet, you have to fight, you can't give up. I'm nothing without you, I'm no one. I may as well let the wyrm drown the world if I lose you because there will be nothing left for me here. Dammit, Scarlet, you stubborn pain in my ass, if you don't shake this off, I'll... I'll..."

Mal ran out of words, something that hadn't happened in recent memory, and he pressed his face into her bark and felt tears prick behind his eyes.

At first he thought that the song he heard was the ache of his own heart. Then he realized it was a voice, and he looked up to find the mermaid, Saina, standing with her legs planted, singing, and there was an unexpected tickle of magic as her voice soared.

Chapter 24

Scarlet was floating.

Pain was a concept she had never understood. She sympathized with it, saw what it did to humans and shifters, but it had always been an abstract; it was a thing that happened to other people, not to her.

Now, she was *all* pain. Pain and poison and darkness. She could feel the salt in her veins, biting into her power, sucking it away.

She wasn't floating, she was sinking, sinking through the earth as she had when Mal had taken her into the depths of the island.

But this time, she was alone and adrift, without Mal's wings folded protectively around her, and she wasn't sure which way was up.

All around her was laughter and a whisper like silk against silk.

Mal? she tried to call. He was so far away.

And someone else answered.

Ah... the tree.

There was a malevolence with her: a terrible, powerful presence that had always been safely below, safely slumbering.

Scarlet could not see, but she could sense great eyes on her, half-lidded. *You were one of the ones who could stop me,* a silvery voice whispered. *The tree and the song. Together with the stone dragon, you could have kept me in my prison, rebuilt my cage around me.*

The song? Scarlet felt like her mind was moving sluggishly, like she was on the verge of understanding something just out of her capability. Everything *hurt.*

She could hear... singing.

Of course! He meant Saina.

Saina was trying to sing the salt from her... but Scarlet knew it was too late, the damage was too deep and it had already hurt her tree too badly. Even if Saina could draw every crystal from her veins, her tree was dying; Scarlet's power was already drained.

She could feel the wyrm grin and suddenly recognized its plan.

You did this on purpose! You're trying to get her to exhaust herself saving me! It had neutralized the two of them in one simple move.

Behind her, there was another set of eyes opening in the darkness.

I don't take chances, the feathered wyrm chuckled from its second head.

This was our third try, the first head admitted. *She resisted the first attempt.*

The second snapped, *You pushed too far, too fast, promised too much.*

The broken mind should have done her job the second time. The first one whined.

It's been undone, somehow. I think the broken mind went back, but we don't know when, the second speculated.

The first head growled. *It's too bright between the broken mind and the stag. We can't always see there.*

Broken mind? *Gizelle!*

The second head smirked, hearing Scarlet's sudden realization. *Such a sweet thing, so trusting. And you did most of the work for me, winning her faith and affection, drawing her out of her safe place. All I had to do was give her your own words, push her to the edge, and then tell her exactly how to fix everything.*

A chorus of voices rose like a storm all around Scarlet, drowning out Saina's far-off song. The dryad would have covered her ears if she'd been able to. It was impossible to pick individual phrases from the chaos.

For you, perhaps, the wyrm scoffed. *I have much more sophisticated minds.*

Scarlet could feel its self satisfaction, its pride.

The broken one merely needed a little direction, a little focus... the wyrm demonstrated, pulling a few of the voices forward, insistent and emotional. Mal's dragon: *She is our treasure. We must get her off this island.* Scarlet heard her own voice: *It's all my fault.*

And the wyrm's voice, thick with kindness and sorrow as its heads circled her: *If you kill the tree, Scarlet will be free... she can go to safety with everyone else... release her from the tree.* You *can fix everything! You can help!*

Scarlet, even knowing what the monster was and the lies it told, was dazzled by the promise in its words.

I have to be careful when the stag can hear us, one of the heads hissed.

Fortunately, he is not always *there,* the other head chuckled.

But when he is... we do not understand why she stops listening, the things she feels, the first pouted.

It is too bright, between them, the second agreed.

How could this all happen so quickly?

Scarlet hadn't meant to ask the question out loud, but the wyrm plucked it effortlessly from her mind.

The broken one can wedge cracks in time. Speed things up, slow them down... It is a curious side effect of her mother's gift, and because she trusts me, she trusts me to control it for her.

Scarlet felt anger rise in her throat. Gentle Gizelle, whose trust was so hard to win, had been fooled into believing that this voice was her friend. How long had it been whispering to the poor young woman, feeding her out-of-context voices, convincing her of its friendship, and using her to its own purpose?

That's what happened to the cage, she realized. *You* aged *it, using Gizelle's magic.*

One of the heads—Scarlet had lost track of which was which—laughed triumphantly. *The spell that trapped me made two foolish assumptions,* it sneered. *The first was that time would flow uniformly, that it was an immutable constant.*

The second? Scarlet asked, afraid of its answer.

That I have been asleep.

Whatever of Scarlet wasn't pain was now fear and she would have flung herself away if she had possessed a body to control.

The wyrm's voice filled the rock around her as both heads spoke. *I have watched, and I have waited, and I have learned, and I have stolen, and the world shall fall before me and know my wrath and I will not rest until I have cleansed the surface of the blight of man and taken back my kingdom.*

Mal will end you, Scarlet cried desperately. *Above the ground or below, he* will *stop you.*

He cannot end me, I am immortal! No one can best me. The wyrm sound more amused than intimidated.

Immortal is not infallible. You've been caged before, Scarlet pointed out. *You can be caged again!*

The wyrm grinned with both of its dire mouths.

But I won't be. The song will end, the tree will fall, and I will be free at last...

Scarlet could hear the desperation in Saina's distant song, the strength bleeding from it as she sang her heart out.

Saina, no...

The music trailed off.

You are alone now, the wyrm told her with hissing satisfaction. *You are powerless and I am all but free and the world will fall before me.*

But he was wrong—at least about one thing.

She *wasn't* alone. She was never truly alone, even in her greatest loneliness.

Trees didn't speak in words.

They spoke in slow impressions of sunlight and rain, in memories of cool earth and whispers of wind. Their words were bright flowers and dark shadows and deep roots and tall, grasping branches.

Scarlet knew them, like humans knew the steady thrum of their own heartbeats and the regular breaths of their own lungs.

If the wyrm had been made of anger and false promise, her trees were made of trust and selfless love.

And as she had devoted herself to them, they repaid it now, giving their own life energy to purge the last of the poison from her tree and reinstate her there.

The wyrm snarled, trying to keep her as her rainforest pulled her gently back.

But it was not in its element, and her trees were patient and strong.

The stone dragon does not have enough power to stop me without you! the wyrm hissed, releasing her contemptuously. *I have still won!*

Scarlet had an impression of a great force, coiling to strike, and then she was standing in a rain of her own petals.

Chapter 25

Mal raged helplessly. "What is the siren doing?" he demanded of no one in particular. He could feel the pull of Saina's magic song, but couldn't figure out what was happening, and it made him feel useless and on edge. It wasn't like his own healing spells, and Scarlet's tree looked worse than ever.

"She's drawing the poison from the tree," Bastian said, watching her almost as anxiously as Mal was. "She did this with me once, with goldshot, and with Wrench, after a snakebite. But this... it's more than she's ever tried to do before."

The dying leaves were starting to shimmer and, after a moment of alarm, Mal realized that they were covered in crystals. Confusion resolved into understanding: they were crystals of salt that Saina was pulling out of the tree through the leaves.

"We're losing her!" Mal said in despair.

"I don't understand," Amber said, shaking her head. Tony had his arms around her. "I don't understand how it could happen so fast. This soil was just disturbed, but it can take weeks for a tree to leech salt up from its roots. It shouldn't have hurt her so badly so quickly."

Graham grunted what Mal assumed was an agreement.

Mal stared at the tree, which was starting to look frosted in the salt crystals, like a great, gorgeous chandelier. It was possible that Scarlet's magic just moved at a faster pace than a normal tree... but the storm had arrived much faster than it ought to as well; the air was already thick with moisture and pressure and the wind was making the crystalized leaves chime together. Red petals were swirling through the air.

When there were problems with time, he knew where to look.

In three swift steps, he closed the distance to Gizelle and took her face in his hand. "What did you do?" he snarled. "What did you do to her?"

Gizelle gave a wordless cry of fear and despair. Mal saw Conall gather himself to attack and locked the Irish elk shifter into stasis with a few quick words and a gesture.

His focus was still on Gizelle. "You *salted* her! You tried to *kill* her! Why would you do this?"

The rest of the staff started to surge forward to protect her but Mal froze them all with a flick of his wrist.

"You told me we had to!" Gizelle wailed. "Your dragon said, *She is our treasure. We must get her off the island*!"

Mal went as rigid as the frozen staff as he recognized his dragon's exact words.

"My friend told me I had to free her from the tree so she wouldn't get hurt!" Gizelle buried her face in her hands. "So many voices, so many places! One of them said this was the only way! Over and over, this was the only way, and there are so many voices and it's *all my fault*!"

"What voice told you this?" Mal demanded in icy suspicion. "This specifically, with the salt and the shovel. What did it sound like?"

"So many voices..." Gizelle moaned. "Gathered up at the end like a sonic wave."

"The voice that told you to put salt on Scarlet," Mal roared at her. "What did it sound like?"

Gizelle looked at him with terror and misery in her eyes. "Rustling feathers..."

Conall, somehow, furiously, was fighting his way forward as if he was moving through honey, his mate-bond overcoming even Mal's spell.

Mal released the spell with a sweep of his hand and let go of the woman. Conall went not for Mal, but for Gizelle, sweeping her into his arms protectively. The rest of the staff staggered in place, not sure what to do with their new freedom and new information.

"So many voices," Gizelle wept hysterically into Conall's shoulder, trembling violently. "Too many! I don't understand how to make sense of it! I want them to end!"

"You gave me sound, beloved," he murmured gently, cradling her close. "Let me give you silence." He closed his eyes and concentrated.

Relief spread over Gizelle's face like a sunrise and she went limp in his arms. "It is quiet at the end, past the wave where voices can't reach," she said, exhausted and she touched her mouth in wonder. Mal guessed she couldn't hear her own spoken words.

He met Conall's angry gaze over Gizelle's head. "If she's been hearing the wyrm..."

A gasp made him turn, just in time to see Saina crumple into Bastian's arms... and Scarlet was suddenly standing among them.

She was solid again, but she was not the Scarlet that Mal knew. Gone were the heels and the timeless business clothes.

Her bright hair was loose and wild around her, and her bare feet were a few inches above the moss. She stood for a moment like this, her eyes like feral emeralds, and Mal climbed to his feet.

"Scarlet," he said helplessly. His dragon seized his heart in careless claws and squeezed the breath from him.

She lives.

Mal knew that he could never lose her again, that he would trade the entire world to save her if that's what it took, and his chest felt like it would crack from the conflict he faced.

She looked at him, her gaze like a million miles, then blinked. She took a breath—her first—and bent her head with great effort, stepping out of the air and back to the earth. As she took that small step, she was somehow smaller, more Scarlet and less elemental. Her hair twisted itself back and she was dressed again, with short heels and a narrow skirt.

The effort it took was palpable and the Scarlet that remained looked tired and weak. Mal did not need to cast power sight to know that her energy had been drained to almost nothing.

"I didn't do that," Saina said hoarsely from Bastian's arms. "I was losing her. I tried, but I couldn't save her. There was... something else."

For a moment, the only sound was the wind, and the chime of salt-heavy leaves falling; Scarlet's tree was nearly bare and the jungle was weirdly still.

"My forest," Scarlet said, swaying in place. "My forest gave itself... there's almost nothing left."

"Scarlet..." Mal was at her side, catching her desperately into his embrace.

She was alarmingly frail in his grasp, a shadow of her former self as she clung to his arms. "Mal," she whispered. "Mal, it's awake. It's been awake. You have to stop it, *now*. This is your chance. I can't help you."

Mal's stomach clenched. "If I go down to fight him now, everyone here on the surface dies."

He had to shout, because the wind was suddenly howling. Scarlet winced as there was a crash in the jungle and one of the huge trees toppled slowly towards into the clearing. It ripped branches from its neighbors and Mal thought the tearing sounds as it fell seemed like screams.

The ground trembled at its fall, though it came down well away from Scarlet's tree. Everyone clung to each other, staring with wide eyes, but the earth didn't stop its growling and shaking as the tree settled.

"More earthquakes?" Jenny said in alarm.

"I don't think this is an earthquake," Travis said, with none of his usual light humor.

"If you don't go down to fight him, far more people die," Scarlet reminded him. "I've met him, Mal. You can't let him go free."

"This is just the edge of the storm," Mal said in despair. "And much worse is to come."

"Can you make one of those fancy portals to somewhere a little safer?" Breck yelled over the whipping wind.

Mal hesitated. The safe places he was familiar with and could portal to were halfway around the world. He should be conserving his magic for the fight that was galloping down on them, but he couldn't leave them here to die. He hadn't realized how much he'd relied on the promise of having Scarlet's magic to draw on.

"You have to save your strength for the fight," Scarlet said miserably, guessing his train of thought. "Can you portal them just to the dock? They can escape on the boat..."

Mal hadn't been to the dock, but he'd been to the pool deck, and he sketched as big a doorway as he dared into the air and brought it to sizzling life. Everyone dashed through, just as a great boom shook the island and Mal felt the cage below the surface explode into shards of broken magic.

They staggered from Scarlet's clearing to a pool deck that was shaking and buckling, tiles popping out as great cracks appeared. Glass everywhere was shattering, furniture from the pool was picked up by wild winds and smashed to the far walls. As they fought to stand on the swaying ground, against the wind, a storm surge rolled in from the angered ocean and buried the dock and the entire beach in swirling foam and crashing waves.

The boat docked there was flung as if it was a child's toy, right into the railing of the pool deck, and it broke into chunks. Some of the pieces bounced back into the roiling water and some flew up to skid over the tiles and splash into the churning pool. One of the motors struck a palm tree that gave a shudder and upended.

"Or not!" Travis said wryly, shouting over the wind.

Laura lost her footing on the heaving ground and Tex caught her before she fell. Mates clung to each other. Several shifted to find better steadiness on four paws, including Chef and Magnolia, who sheltered others from the wind behind their massive bears.

For a moment, the earth stilled slightly and the wind was a little less, but Mal knew that it was only a matter of time before the wyrm fought his way to the surface.

"You have to get out of here now," he said in despair. He couldn't save Scarlet, but he could save the people who were loyal to her. Scarlet stepped back from him, swaying weakly in place. He started to sketch a new doorway, focusing on his stronghold in New York. It would take a reckless amount of energy, but he knew he had to do it. The earth was starting to rumble again as the wyrm crawled for the surface; they didn't have more than a few minutes.

"Wait!" It was Graham, stepping forward with Alice's hand in his own. "You could have beat it with Scarlet's power, right?"

"I don't have anything left," Scarlet said helplessly.

The gardener ignored her, glaring at Mal in challenge. "Corbin... he could use a shifter's energy to do magic. Could you do that with us?"

Mal stared at him. "Bind *you*? You're just..."

"All of us. If you could tap all of our power, would it be enough?" Graham looked aside at Alice, and she set her jaw and stepped closer to him, nodding in agreement.

"I've never had a chance to save the world before," she said merrily.

Mal swept his gaze over the assembled shifters and gestured carefully. They all glowed with power—if not the scope of Scarlet's single-handed energy, each with their own unique strength—and strongest of all were the mate-bonds between them, a curious glow of magic and love. "I could do that," he realized in astonishment. Graham and Alice both stood open to him, the simple act of their offer putting their potential in his hands.

This wasn't magic the way that he had studied it, with spells and structure and study. This was something more elemental, like his innate ability to slip through rock, or Scarlet's ability to make things grow. "This could work," he said, with something painfully like hope growing in his gut.

Bastian, just behind Alice, exchanged a look with Saina and moved to stand beside Graham with her. "I'm not Scarlet's caliber, but I *am* a dragon," he said proudly.

Mal hadn't banished his energy sight and it was as if a veil had fallen away from Bastian's source.

Scarlet put a trembling hand to her mouth, tears shining in her eyes.

"I'm nearly tapped," Saina said, coming to Bastian's side. "But what I've got, I'd give." She was a gentle light, even exhausted.

Darla and Breck came forward, hand in hand. "We're not going to let you have all that fun without us," Breck called over a gust of wind.

"I got a debt to pay back," Wrench said to Lydia, and she lifted her chin proudly and met Mal's gaze with a firm nod.

Magnolia and Chef, still in bear form, bowed their great heads in agreement.

It was Mary who dragged Neal forward. "We're in."

Tony gave Scarlet a conflicted look and Amber spoke his concerns aloud. "Could this hurt our child?"

Mal felt like he'd been sideswiped by the offers, his power sight nearly overwhelmed. "I don't think so," he said, dazedly. "The data I've seen suggests that *in vitro* exposure to magic may cause children to shift earlier, but I've never seen evidence of harm. I would not take enough to hurt any of you."

"Then I'm in," Amber said with a lift of her chin.

"*Pura vida*," Tony said. *Pure life*, the Costa Rican motto. Their magic was suddenly at his fingertips.

"Us, too," Tex and Laura said in unison.

Jenny shifted from the otter form she'd taken shelter in. "Is it a conflict of interest if we have to face each other in the courtroom later?"

"I will preemptively concede every case to you," Mal said, a hint of a smile at his mouth.

The smile died as the subtle rumble of the earth beneath them intensified.

"We're with you," Jenny said swiftly. "Do you need something more than that?"

"You'd all do this?" Mal said in astonishment, looking at the assembled shifters who had gathered forward. "You'd take this risk?"

"Not for *you*," Graham growled. "And maybe not for the world. But we'd do it for Scarlet."

Chapter 26

Scarlet was the only one of the group who wasn't soaking wet, so nothing could hide the tears tracking down her face. She didn't try to wipe them away.

She understood the depth of what each of them was offering, she knew the trust it took, and it left her awed and honored.

Conall had been standing back with Gizelle curled in his arms. Scarlet wasn't sure whether he could hear any of what was happening, or if he understood it, until he stepped forward, glaring at Mal.

"What do you have to do?" he asked.

Gizelle rolled out of his embrace and landed on her feet, nearly falling to her knees on the unsteady tile. "I can't run," she said in alarm, looking up at Conall.

"And I won't run without you," Conall told her firmly.

"You have us," Gizelle said to Mal gravely. Then she looked up at Conall. "But I have to do something first!" she said wildly, and she bolted to stand in front of Saina and stare into her eyes for a long moment.

Saina shook her head in confusion and then Gizelle was dashing back to hold onto Conall's hand and nod at Mal.

Scarlet remembered the wyrm's cryptic talk: *It was undone, somehow. I don't know when.*

167

Mal closed his eyes and everyone gave a sudden intake of breath. Scarlet, her own power cold and banked inside, could still sense the swell of magic in her mate. It was a muddier magic than her own, or even than Mal's innate earth dragon magic, but it was as solid.

I can do this, she heard him say in a sudden burst of hope. Then she felt his laughter like a caress. We *can do this*, he corrected.

It wasn't any too soon; the long, low growl of the ground beneath them was a crescendo and they were having to dance in place for balance. Gravel rattled and some of the remaining glass shattered in place as the earth began to shake in earnest.

Mal fixed his eyes on the ground and Scarlet touched his arm, knowing he wanted to dive into the earth and stop the monster now, while he still had some advantage. He turned and pulled her into a last, damp embrace.

Whatever you have to do... Scarlet started sincerely, thinking of her helpless tree.

I won't drain them, Mal said fiercely. *I will be able to release them before the end, if it comes to that.*

He kissed her once, briefly and hard, then pushed her away. "Take what shelter you can," he commanded over the sound of the rising wind. "The bar may stand."

The shifters gathered themselves and fled up the shivering stairs, just as the gathering clouds opened up and rain began to pelt down on them.

The rain changed to hail before they were all under the overhanging restaurant deck, first pebble-sized, then fist-sized, then chunks of ice the size of small melons were hurtling towards them at impossible speeds. Tex and Travis toppled the cooler onto its side to act as a defense against the onslaught while some of them hid behind of the bar. Magnolia and Chef, still in their bear forms, protected others, thick fur ruffled in the wind.

Unable to help them, barely able to keep her physical form, Scarlet stood at the edge of the bar deck, watching her resort tremble as Mal began to chant in earnest. The runes on his forearms were bright in the gathering darkness.

The hail gave way to rain, heavy and driving. Scarlet stared through the gloom to where Mal was beginning to weave the tools he needed to subdue the monster long enough to cage it.

Shimmering ropes appeared, looping around the cottages and across the pool deck, and Scarlet wasn't sure if they were shivering with energy, or from the endless shaking of the earth. It was starting to feel almost normal, the earthquake had gone on so long.

Then, as if challenging that idea, it intensified and someone screamed as one of the columns cracked and a portion of the restaurant deck collapsed. Further away, Scarlet could hear building and trees groan in protest, and more glass was shattering.

Mal leaped into the air, spreading tiger's eye wings, just as the wyrm emerged from beneath one of Scarlet's cottages, throwing rock and earth out of its path.

Each of its heads was a wedge nearly the size of Mal's entire dragon, its great eyes lighting white above a snarling mouth full of shining teeth. Coils of his legless body flattened another cottage, and his tail sent white gravel spitting in all directions as it sliced up through the resort paths.

Scarlet had expected the wyrm's size, but she hadn't expected the creature's unearthly beauty. The serpentine body was most similar to a snake, but moved in ways that no snake could ever manage, flowing and pulsing in shimmering waves. Its gleaming body was covered from face to tail-tip in razor-tipped iridescent blue and green feathers, each one reflective and flexible enough to move like a leaf. They sang like tuned windchimes with every sinuous movement.

It was like watching music, shimmering waves of color blazing from its feathered hide.

Mal rose up into the storm and fell down upon him like a sparrow on an alligator, the runes on his dragon's forelegs glowing as he folded his wings and dropped. Magic-strengthened, he hit the wyrm right behind the nearest head, driving it down to the earth as the ropes whipped up to capture one of its long necks.

The second head dove for the golden dragon, snapping down... on a brilliant blue shield that snapped to life. Through the driving, pounding sound of the storm, Scarlet could hear the teeth screech off of the barrier. The first head was ripping up from the ropes holding it, straining and pulling as the second head changed its tactic and rammed into Mal with all of its strength.

A portal opened behind him, another opening directly above him with the same sweep of his tail, and then Mal was dropping into one and out of the other to dive onto the head flailing through empty space. Claws that gleamed blue light drove through the slithering feathers. The first head had fought its way free of the magical rope and was snapping at Mal in fury.

The wyrm, now free, twisted in a corkscrew into the air like it was climbing an invisible ladder and scraped along Mal's hide with a sound like metal on stone.

That was when Scarlet realized that the plumage wasn't merely decorative. Every gleaming blue-green feather was knife-edged, and strong enough that she felt scale slice beneath it.

Mal, she whispered, staggered by his pain.

She could feel the spell that healed the cuts, and see the runes flare briefly on the dragon's forearms. Flexible as a cat, he twisted away, vanished through a portal, and reappeared above the wyrm once again.

One of its heads turned to snap at him, the other ducked to come up behind him, but Mal dove between them, then made a mid-air turn that no bird would have attempted and came up under one of the chins, digging in with magic-hardened claws as he hauled it back down toward the magical ropes wriggling above the resort below.

The other head screamed and came crashing in against Mal's blazing shield.

Chapter 27

This isn't anything we haven't trained for, Mal told his dragon as they tumbled through another portal to get behind the wyrm again. They both knew he was desperately lying.

The magic from the Shifting Sands staff was nearly as strong as Scarlet's had been. But it was incoherent, competitive, and using magic that wasn't his was just different enough than using his own that he was sometimes scrambling to understand what he was doing. His shields were a moment slower than they needed to be, his portals just a little sloppier. His concentration was broken between smoothing the lines of power and setting the spells, all while he fought an angry, razor-feathered, two-headed wyrm who had everything to lose and vengeance to gain... in the middle of a raging storm.

He felt like a boy again, a dragon who could barely fly, in the air being pitted against experienced warriors with the advantage of fire.

We won those battles, his dragon reminded him, dodging a head followed by a swirling blender of sharp feathers. *Sometimes.*

Mal could hear his father's voice. *What edge do you always have?*

Knowledge. What did he know that could possibly help him?

You know nothing, a voice intruded scornfully.

Less than nothing, a second voice chimed.

Then, together, W*e have all the* edgessssss.

The wyrm cackled in unison at its own joke as it sent the tail that Mal had lost track of to twist around him in a swirl of dark, iridescent feathers. Mal gave a roar of pain, failing in surprise to raise a shield before they sliced into the scales along his side, through the magic-hardening spell altogether. He was poorly positioned for a portal. The driving rain and wind made it difficult to stay steady long enough to accurately dive through a small one and a large one took more power.

A swift healing spell kept the cuts from being deadly, but Mal was keenly aware that he was burning through the magical reserves at an unsustainable rate.

He steeled himself for a phased attack, dropping through a portal just a little above from one of the great heads as he escaped snapping jaws. He took hold of the huge wedge head and used a jolt of magic that burned like alcohol through his veins to drag the wyrm with him back to where the ropes waited to capture it. The other head and the tail twisted to batter against his gleaming shield.

They fought, teeth shrieking over shield, claws digging through feathers, magic will against brute strength and fury.

Harder and deeper, Mal poured the magic that had been given to him selflessly into all of the spells he was keeping alive: the shield, the force dragging them towards the shining ropes he was keeping alive and waiting, the magic hardening of his claws and scales.

For one bright moment, he thought he could do it; one strong push and he could force the wyrm down to his destiny.

But then the wyrm flared every feather in braking power and the free head opened its toothy jaws to roar a command into the storm. Furious wind tore through the shield to Mal's wings, ripping the membrane. The rain was so dense that it blinded him and Mal, unable to divert any magic to healing, shivered in pain.

The wyrm took advantage of his distraction and crashed into his shield with its tail, overpowering it with sheer force. Mal clung to the head under his claws desperately; he couldn't portal in this kind of wind, and he didn't dare let go, even as the spell pulling the wyrm back to be caged unraveled in the air and the wyrm slithered back up into the clouds.

Then the second head bit into him and ripped him loose, tossing him end over end into the storm.

For a moment, Mal only tumbled, helpless and stunned. Then he cast a swift healing spell to stem the worst of the bleeding and he tried to make sense of where he was and where the wyrm was.

Out of the cloud and rain, a grinning head came sweeping with jaws wide to snap at his ravaged wings. Mal dived for a portal, missed it in the driving wind, and slammed into the body of the wyrm beyond.

Landing in feathers was somehow less comfortable than it sounded when the feathers were tipped in knives.

Mal kicked off and fell backwards through the clouds until he could spread his wings and fly again with his damaged wings.

Think! he berated himself. *Act! Fight!* His magic stores were draining too quickly, and he couldn't risk harming the shifters who had so selflessly given it to him.

The wyrm spiraled down towards him, lazily, and batted at him with a playful tail.

It was a game, Mal realized as he dodged the tail with effort and feathers skidded off a hasty shield when he wasn't quite fast enough. The wyrm was toying with him, confident in its victory now.

Their battle, swiftly becoming one-sided, was taking them out over the storm-raged jungle and Mal had a sudden cold moment of terror. Was the wyrm deliberately taking them to Scarlet's grove?

The tree... one of the heads hissed dismissively, as if it felt his thought. *We stopped the tree.*

She is powerless, the other smirked.

To Mal's horror, the storm was effortlessly flattening the giant trees of the rain forest below them, ripping them up by their roots and tossing them aside as if they were tiny saplings. He had a glimpse of the clearing, just beyond.

Scarlet...

Mal closed his eyes and dug as deep into the magic as he dared, waiting until the two baleful heads were close together and then casting a shield not over himself, but over the wyrm's two heads, like throwing a bag over two squirming snakes.

He had only a heartbeat of optimism before the two heads, growling, moved in opposite directions and ripped the shield into a spray of sparks.

Before we take the world back, we will make you suffer, the wyrm snarled in harmony. *We will make you pay the sins of your forefathers in the blood we draw from your sides and the pain we will make you scream.*

But when Mal expected the feathered creature to rip his heart out by upending Scarlet's tree, it only growled into the storm and the wind sent him tumbling as the wyrm chased him like a cat chasing a crippled mouse.

Mal spread badly damaged wings, breathing what he knew was his last healing spell into them as he fled back towards the ocean, hoping only to draw the monster and the storm it was making from Scarlet's unprotected grove.

Chapter 28

Scarlet had never felt so helpless. Not as a new dryad, not wandering the streets in England with her dying tree. Not when she was most sure she would lose her resort. Not even feeling her tree's life slip away after she had been salted.

Her forest was tapped, the life energy that they had shared with her so selflessly drained to nothing. Even if they survived the storm and captured the wyrm, she didn't know if the jungle would ever thrive again.

And there was nothing she could do for her mate.

She stood at the edge of the bar deck, as if she could do anything to protect the staff hiding there. They were crouched behind whatever shelter they could find—toppled tables, chunks of rubble from the restaurant deck above.

And above them was the terrible aerial battle, half obscured by charcoal clouds and blowing debris.

The wyrm tore chunks from Mal's hide, ripped at the webbing of his wings, batting him out of the sky like he was nothing more than a minor inconvenience. Every time, Mal returned to try to drag it back, every time more slowly. Bright shields flared more briefly with each hit.

He was being idly savaged, Scarlet realized. The only reason that the wyrm hadn't left the island for its freedom yet was to exact painful revenge from Mal himself, playing with him like a cat with its helpless prey. Mal's magic was finite, his ability to heal was slowing and his protections were failing.

Bastian was suddenly standing beside her. "He's released us," he said, sounding weary.

Scarlet felt her chest seize with pain. Mal had only his own magical reserves remaining, and she knew they would not last long.

It was still raining, still windy, but the worst of it was away over the jungle, beating on her forest and battering Mal.

Bastian went to the edge of the deck; the railing was drunken on the cracked concrete.

Saina staggered to him against the wind. "What are you doing?"

"I'm going to go fight with him," Bastian said matter-of-factly. "He isn't going to save the world alone."

Saina gave a low keen of misery and dragged his face down to hers for a long kiss. Then she released him. "I will sing for you," she said. "As long as I have voice."

Then Bastian was rising on his green wings into the buffeting wind.

"I wish there was something we could do," Jenny said, shifting from otter to woman at Scarlet's side.

"He could have used more of our magic," Travis said, soaking wet at her side.

"He didn't want to drain you too far," Scarlet said miserably.

Mal and Bastian looked like tiny songbirds trying to harass a great roc. A great, angry, confident roc.

Saina was singing what little power she had left into her mate with a hoarse voice against the grasping wind.

Scarlet cringed. Even that was her fault. If Saina had not exhausted herself saving the dryad... If she had not *been* a dryad, Mal would have been able to evacuate everyone and fight the battle where he could beat it.

Scarlet thought bitterly. *It's all my fault*!

Gizelle, crouching behind a table near Conall, looked up at her abruptly, as if she'd heard Scarlet's thought. Her white-streaked hair was dripping wet and tangled, and Scarlet wondered how many ways she had failed the young woman. She should have persuaded Conall to take her off the island earlier. She should have taken the threat that slept—didn't sleep—below them more seriously.

Scarlet dragged her eyes up to the storm.

Mal and Bastian gamely fought, but no one on the ground had any illusions that they had a chance against the beast.

Jenny couldn't watch after only a few moments, turning to bury her face in Travis' chest.

"It's just toying with them," Travis said quietly.

Jenny looked up. "If it really wanted to hurt Mal, why hasn't it gone for Scarlet's tree?" she asked quietly.

"It doesn't think I'm important anymore," Scarlet guessed, remembering the wyrm's confusion over the bond that Gizelle and Conall shared. "It doesn't understand love, or loyalty. Because I have no power, it thinks Mal doesn't care for me any further."

She knew love. And loyalty... she only had to think about the staff of Shifting Sands and everything they'd done for her. They'd offered up their own shifter energy. They'd even pooled their resources to *buy* her the island.

Scarlet froze.

Mal! she cried, knowing the risk of distracting him. *Mal, you have to sell me the island!*

The wyrm twisted beneath him, the razor edges of his feathers slicing up into Mal's claws. Mal roared in pain, but pressed his assault, futilely trying to drive the wyrm back down with Bastian's help. *I'm a little busy for a real estate transaction*, he pointed out. His voice was not defeated, though he must surely recognize his inevitable loss of this game.

There was no time to explain. *Trust me*, Scarlet begged. *Shift and accept my offer for the island so I can help you. Aloud, with witnesses. There can be no doubts.*

She could feel his hesitation as he considered. The storm was rising to an impossible tenor, the wyrm was driving him back up into the clouds. He'd be more vulnerable yet in his human form.

But he *trusted* her.

The jaws of one of the heads snapped in air as Mal unexpectedly streaked away from the battle, retreating to the battered resort.

Bastian swooped down at the creature's tail, sending a blast of flame over the wyrm that simply rolled off its shimmering feathers. But the attack made the wyrm hesitate, and that was enough time for Mal to streak over the jungle, drop from the sky and shift to human long enough to shout over the wind, "I accept your offer for the island before these witnesses with no exceptions or refusals!"

He gave Scarlet a piercing look. "I hope you know what you're doing," he told her, then he was launching into the violent air again just as the wyrm got its teeth around one of Bastian's rear legs mid-air and Saina screamed helplessly.

It was enough.

Scarlet felt the contract that had walled her from the far half of the island dissolve with Mal's words, and all that had been there was suddenly *hers*.

She could feel every inch of the island, every ridge and rock and beach.

The forest there was not as vital as her half of the island had been, not nurtured as hers had been by a dryad of great power for many decades, but it was thick and *alive*, and when she reached out for it, it answered.

Wild jungle covered most of the island, and even the blades of grass where tame lawn had been gave her a little tickle of awareness. The arboretum at Beehag's compound had housed dozens of rare trees, their dormant energy buzzing awake as she caressed them with her greeting.

You are my forest now, she told them lovingly, and from the smallest sapling to the greatest giant kapok, they answered with devotion and delight.

Power coursed through her once more, nearly as strong as it had ever been, filling all the empty corners of her tree.

And she knew exactly what to do with it.

As Mal battled against the wind to rejoin the fight, he went incandescent with the magic that Scarlet abruptly flung at him. His golden claws struck fast and true, magic-strengthened. The wyrm gave a cry of rage and pain as the claws managed to penetrate his armor-like feathers, dropping his hold on Bastian's leg.

The green dragon fell away from the battle with a final jet of flame and tumbled into a shallow glide to land in the turbulent pool, shifting into human form as he hit the surface and sank.

Saina left the questionable shelter of the rubble of the bar, scrambled down the broken steps and dived fearlessly after him, nearly falling as the wind howled against her.

Scarlet had no attention to spare for them, or for any of the people she loved as dearly. All of her focus was on the battle above as she coiled in wait.

Chapter 29

Mal felt his exhaustion burn away as Scarlet—his amazing, brilliant Scarlet—re-filled his wells of magic with her pure, elemental power. He was going to pay for this soon enough, he knew, but the important thing was that he had it *now*. He had a chance again to fulfill his destiny.

The wyrm was not convinced of that truth, snarling and fighting with all its considerable strength against Mal's claws.

You cannot beat me, one of the heads snarled.

I do not have to beat you, Mal retorted. Not by himself.

They were in the belly of the storm now, and Mal's wings could not keep him steady in the raging winds. But he wasn't trying to fly, he wasn't even trying to fight. He wrapped a strong tail around the wyrm's throat and let himself tumble towards the ground with sudden, enchanted mass, dragging his adversary with him as the feathers scraped uselessly on Mal's magic-hardened scales.

They didn't fall for long; the wyrm was stronger than Mal's dead weight, and its surprise at Mal's action didn't last.

But they didn't have to fall far.

They had been fighting high over the tops of the whipping trees of the island, Mal trying hard not to think of Scarlet's tree and the damage it must be taking as huge branches and whole trees were pulled up into the maelstrom.

Now they were just brushing those treetops and as the wyrm gathered itself to spring higher and unleash his anger from above, the rainforest itself came to life.

Green vines whipped up into the storm and wrapped themselves around the sinuous feathered creature. He broke them easily at first, verdant leaves spiraling up into his storm, but more followed, and more, and more, folding down his feathers, dragging him down into the upper canopy, where thick branches stretched and grew into giant, grasping fingers.

The wyrm thrashed, uprooting entire trees and snapping branches, but the sheer number of trees against him saw him pinned, utterly unable to break free. His wind howled, and his rain drove hard against them, but the jungle was unified against him, and Mal set himself into a dive from above.

Ignoring the wind that tore at his scales, Mal set himself upon the wyrm, driving it further down towards the earth. He roared the names of the runes into the storm and the marks on his front legs flared with power as the bars of the new cage rose from the earth to meet them.

The wyrm, thrashing now like a pinned snake, gave a cry of desperate fury. His wind raged, ripping trees from their roots and smashing them down in every direction. His feathers sliced into thick trunks and severed branches.

Mal wasn't sure where they were, how close they were to Scarlet's vulnerable tree, but he made a split-second hesitation at the thought of it.

The hesitation broke his concentration and, for a moment, the wyrm was free. It slipped between the half-formed bars to slither towards the resort itself.

Mal wasn't sure if it was seeking a place with fewer trees to hold it, or if he knew the value of the shifters huddled in the ruins to the combatants and hoped to use them as hostages. Mal was after him again in a heartbeat as he coiled out of the jungle and smashed through the cottages that were still standing. Broken glass and roof tiles swirled up into the wind, bouncing harmlessly off of Mal as he blocked the wyrm's escape to the sky with a shield more vast than any he had ever managed before.

Trees exploded up from the ground and potted plants burst their vessels as they instantly grew and grasped at the two-headed wyrm, tying it to the ground.

Mal spoke the words of power again and dropped down onto the wyrm, pressing it down into the earth again as the glimmering bars rose up around them.

The wyrm thrashed and the ground shook and rumbled from the force of its struggle.

A scream made Mal realize that the battered restaurant was beginning to groan and collapse and Scarlet's ragged staff fled from the bar where they'd been sheltered.

The wyrm, in one final, vindictive effort, chose the most helpless of the creatures before it, and sucked in breath for a last blast of wind.

"Get down!" Scarlet cried in a great voice. "Hold on!" All of them automatically dropped to the shivering ground to cover their heads from the flying debris...

...All of them except Conall, who was not touching Gizelle and could not hear the warning.

Scarlet's shroud of greenery rose moments too late; the wyrm's gust caught the musician square in the chest and swept him backwards into the crumbling building.

The musician hit one of the columns, so hard that the terrible crunch of his breaking bones was louder than the storm. Jagged pieces of the restaurant deck rained down like hail over his still form.

Mal did not have to wonder if he had survived the impact; Gizelle's scream of agony and loss would haunt his dreams forever: a thin wail of despair that threaded the music of the storm like a harmony.

The wyrm, mistakenly thinking that this distraction had bought it escape, made another bid for freedom, to face Mal bristling in new rage.

We will cage you again and bury you deep! his dragon swore. *We will fulfill our destiny!*

You are nothing! the wyrm snarled.

You cannot defeat us! the other head protested.

The feathered wyrm struck out with its tail, and the earth shuddered and groaned, but when it tried to lift it for a second strike, there were new trees and bushes pinning it, its entire body and both necks were being wrapped in leaves and branches like a great green cast as Scarlet unleashed her forest on him.

The storm continued to rage, but the monster was caught.

Mal landed and shifted to human form to perform the final stages of the cage.

Chapter 30

The wyrm snarled, struggling against the vines that were rising from the island. The gleaming bars Mal was building around it were semi-transparent and too far apart to hold it in, but as he chanted, the cage began to solidify and condense upon the captured monster.

Scarlet, concentrating fiercely on keeping the creature subdued and already distracted by another task, was suddenly surprised as something small dashed beside her down the steps to where Mal was facing the feathered heads.

"Gizelle, no!"

Scarlet's first thought was that Gizelle was mad with grief and wanted revenge on the creature that had killed Conall. "Gizelle, wait!"

But the slight woman wasn't trying to get through the bars of the cage to the wyrm in some fit of rage, she was leaping at Mal.

"No!" the gazelle shifter cried, clinging to his arm and covering his runes. "Stop! You have to stop!"

"I have to do this," Mal said, trying to pull away from her without harming her. His teeth were gritted and Scarlet could feel the strain he was under; already he had burned through too much of the magical stores she'd refilled, and she could feel the underlying exhaustion. "Gizelle, it's not a person, it's a creature of destruction!"

The bars of the cage wavered with his distraction.

Scarlet had half her mind on the forest wrapping the wyrm, re-growing vines and grasping trees as fast as his sharp-edged feathers could cut through them. She flickered to Gizelle's side, prepared to try to draw her away. "Gizelle..."

"You can't do this!" Gizelle's voice was big compared to her little frame, wavering but firm.

"I don't have a choice," Mal said between gritted teeth. The runes on his forearms flared, his concentration divided.

"No!" Gizelle wept. "No one deserves to be in a cage!"

She gave up trying to stop Mal and before Scarlet realized what she was doing, Gizelle had darted between the big bars of the cage to face the wyrm.

Scarlet cried out as the wyrm twisted and opened two sets of giant jaws in Gizelle's direction, tearing from her trees. "Gizelle, no!" She lost her grip on the vines she was controlling and was suddenly... somewhere else.

She was standing in knee-deep grass, brilliantly lit by nothing at all. Above her, the sky was featureless black: no stars, no sun, no color.

Gizelle stood with her back straight, her slim gazelle shivering at her side. Mal was here, too, his golden dragon towering above his human form, both of them looking around in curious wonder.

And the wyrm was with them, fluttering its blue and green feathers in confusion. It had no human self beside it.

Mal gestured, and spoke a few words that Scarlet didn't catch, but nothing happened. The wyrm opened his mouths as if he would spit his wind at them... but the grass continued to wave peacefully.

Suspiciously, Scarlet reached out with her own power, calling on the grass to grow... and found that nothing answered.

Gizelle was walking fearlessly forward towards it. "You can run here, always," she said to it, sounding weary and worn down. It thrashed in fury, but despite its great size, it seemed incapable of harm. When it screamed, even the sound seemed powerless.

Gizelle turned her back on it, facing Mal and Scarlet. "No one belongs in a cage," she repeated. "Not even that. Better that he stay here, forever and never, until the sky goes dark."

The wyrm suddenly shifted forms and was a human, with silky, rainbow-dark hair, dressed in soft feathers in peacock blues and greens. "Gizelle," it said coaxingly. "I have always been your friend. Free me and I will make you a queen! We will make the whole world a place to run and you will rule at my side."

Scarlet made a small noise of anger and dismay and Mal said flatly, "Don't listen to it, Gizelle. It was never your friend."

Gizelle turned to regard the wyrm again, ignoring both of them.

"I was Conall's queen," she said mournfully.

"I can bring him back," the wyrm whispered temptingly in a new voice, stepping close to Gizelle. "I brought him down, and I can bring him back, but only if you free me. Let me go from this place and you will be together again."

Scarlet could see the quiver in Gizelle's frame, the hesitation. "No..." she whispered.

"He lies," Mal told Gizelle firmly. "No one can do that."

Scarlet bit her lip.

Gizelle turned and looked at them each in turn and then faced the wyrm again. "You've always spoken nicely to me, and for a long time, I thought that *nice* meant *good*. But you would hurt so many people, and cause so much pain. Even Conall isn't worth that price. I couldn't be that selfish." She stepped closer to it, trembling and fearless at once. "I'm sorry for your hatred and your hunger for destruction. I'm sorry for all your time in a cage, awake and angry. I don't know if you are capable of happiness, but here there will be no time and you will not suffer."

The wyrm seemed to gather itself and Scarlet took a step forward to protect Gizelle—if she even needed protecting in this place—and saw Mal do the same.

Then they were suddenly outside again, the storm still whipping around them as they faced the monstrous form of the half-caged wyrm.

The creature was weirdly still, every feather frozen in space; it was the only thing not moving in the wind. Even small rocks skidded across the tiles in the gale.

"We will have to close the door completely," Mal said, looking at Gizelle in awe. "He will find a way out, if we leave even the tiniest crack. You'll never be able to go back."

Gizelle's shoulders drooped, but she nodded. "I knew that," she said simply. "But I am done running. Nothing matters that much anymore." The tearless grief in her face was like a great weight and Scarlet hurt for her.

"He is immortal and can never die," Mal said gravely. "He will be locked in your place forever in that single moment and I will bury his earthly body. Close the door, Gizelle."

She looked up at him with trusting eyes. "I don't know how."

Chapter 31

Mal gazed down at Gizelle. So much of what she did was instinct, in sharp contrast to his own carefully learned, orderly methods. "I think I can help you," he offered. "I need a physical anchor. Something that means a lot to you would be best, but anything will do."

Gizelle's glance flickered up to the bar deck, where Conall's body lay half-covered in rubble.

"What about this?"

Mal turned to find that Bastian and Saina had climbed from the crumbling pool, and the dragon shifter, looking rather worse for the wear and leaning heavily on his mate, was holding out an ugly, battered piece of metal.

"I found it when we were fleeing back from Scarlet's tree," the lifeguard explained. "My treasure sense went nuts and I had to pick it up."

Gizelle gave a sigh. "Yes," she said.

Mal took it, hefting it in his hand. It was a big chunk of metal, clearly a mechanical lock of some kind that had been badly damaged. A hole had been drilled in it, and a carabiner was looped through that hole. A lock had good symbolism, and when he cast his power sight on it—wincing at the effort it took—he was stunned by the emotions it had captured: Neal's anger and helplessness, Gizelle's fears and confusion... and Conall's deep love.

"This is perfect," he agreed. He put it in Gizelle's hands. "I want you to picture a large door."

She closed her eyes obediently.

"Now imagine a deadbolt—do you know what that is?"

Gizelle nodded.

"Good. Imagine that you've closed the door, and now you're locking it. The lock is heavy, like this, and you can hear it shooting home. You might have to press on the door to make the lock fit. And then nothing can get in or out, forever."

"It's the end," Gizelle said quietly.

Mal didn't need to cast his power sight to confirm her success; Gizelle's hair suddenly shimmered to pure white and the feathered wyrm bleached of color as if it had turned into pale marble.

Forever.

"You did it," Mal murmured to Gizelle.

Scarlet, the same exhaustion in her shoulders that Mal felt on his own, let the vines and trees wrapping the creature go slack and turned to account for the rest of her staff. They began to emerge from the rubble they had used as cover as the storm, no longer powered by the wyrm's wrath, began to die. It was still raining, but was a gentle rain, warm and apologetic.

Two bears, one white and one golden brown, rose to four feet and shook rubble and rain off of them as staff who had sheltered behind them dazedly dusted themselves off.

Gizelle lifted a face tracked with tears and raindrops to look at Mal. "Why am I still here? I don't remember this..."

"The door is closed," Mal said wearily. "You're locked to one time now, like all of us. No more whispers from the future, only memories of the past."

She made a wordless noise of agony and turned away. "I don't want to be here. I thought it would *end* when the door shut."

She slipped around Mal and climbed up the shattered stairs to where Conall's body lay crumpled, her white hair a tangled cloak behind her. Jenny let go of Travis to follow her, and after a moment, Lydia gave Wrench a squeeze and trailed after.

Slowly, weary and battered, they all picked their way one by one and two by two through the rubble, standing in a stunned group on the broken tile to gather around Conall.

Mal, feeling empty and exhausted as never before, stood alone for a moment on the bar level.

"Can you heal him?" Scarlet demanded quietly, suddenly at his side.

"He's dead," Mal told her. "I can't do anything about that."

"I know *that*," Scarlet said impatiently. "Can you *heal* him?"

"It wouldn't do any good," Mal said gently. Should he be flattered that she thought him capable of that? He was too *tired* to feel flattered.

"You have got to stop making assumptions," she replied with a sigh. "I do not have dominion over earth, Mal."

"You're a dryad..." he started.

"And do you see me throwing rocks around or making mountains move?" Scarlet asked scathingly. "Was I even slightly comfortable underground? Did I have any luck controlling dirt? Just because my roots are in earth doesn't mean I don't need air, or fire from the sun, or water from the rain. I don't have any power over dirt or rocks, I make things *grow*."

Mal scowled at her in confusion, trying to make sense of what she was trying to tell him.

"My dominion is *life*, Mal. I can bring Conall back, but it won't do more than make him suffer needlessly and die again if he can't also be healed."

"You can..."

"I can bring him back to life," she said calmly, as if she was not offering the impossible.

"You're sure?"

"I caught him as he died," Scarlet explained. "And I have only been able to hold him here this long because of his bond with Gizelle. We have to hurry, or I will lose him entirely."

"I can heal him," Mal said, testing his wells of power cautiously. They were badly drained, and his ability to control it was nearly burned out completely. He had never strained himself like this before, never even dreamed of controlling so much energy. There were a few swirls of magic left and just enough strength in his mind. "I can do that much."

"Do it then." Scarlet took his hand and they walked slowly up to where Gizelle was lying curled against Conall's still side. Lydia and Jenny were sitting on either side of her, offering mute comfort and the rest of the staff was in a loose, grieving semicircle around them. They had pulled most of the rubble off of Conall, and tried to lay him out in a less unnatural position.

Scarlet took her hand back, but didn't gesture or chant. She only looked at the fallen shifter and Mal didn't understand that she was using her power until Conall suddenly took a shuddering breath, groaned, and began to die from his injuries once more.

Gizelle gave a frightened squeak of alarm, shrinking away. "Conall!"

Jenny stood and stepped back, nearly colliding with Scarlet, and Lydia reached for Gizelle and clasped her hand, murmuring a prayer.

The rest of the staff gasped and whispered and swore in surprise.

Mal cursed and brought his scattered thoughts to bear, naming the runes as he gestured to them. Conall's body arched as the last tattered remains of Mal's magic knit his bones back together and mended crushed organs. He had underestimated the amount of damage the man had taken, and for a bad moment he feared he wouldn't be able to do as he'd promised.

Then Scarlet's pure power was bolstering him again, flowing into him like water after terrible thirst.

Life, her power was *life*.

Her entire forest, now both sides of the island, gave her a deep wellspring of energy without even trying.

Mal would have laughed, if he had the energy left for it. It all made so much sense.

Then Conall began to cough and rolled to one side with a moan of pain. Gizelle reached for him, weeping and shaking.

"I can't... hear..." he said breathlessly, when her hands were on him. "No, I can... but it's so *quiet*."

"The door is shut," Gizelle said simply, laying her head on his shoulder. "I only hear things that are *now*."

Mal couldn't stand any longer, every muscle in his body trembled as badly as Gizelle ever had, and he felt like he had worked his brain into the same kind of weak exhaustion. He could not have managed the most basic of portals or simplest of power sights. He could barely handle the effort of his own thoughts.

He sat down in his tracks, and he might have fallen over on his side, but Scarlet was suddenly behind him, holding him cradled in her arms. The scent of her damp hair swirling around him made him feel utterly, completely safe.

We are *safe*, his dragon told him, feeling equally stretched thin. *We are safe and we have fulfilled our destiny and our mate will protect us while we rest.*

It wasn't the destiny that Mal had come to Shifting Sands expecting, and he didn't have answers for their future: Would he move his hoard from New York? Would she agree to marry him, or was she too independent to accept such an earthly conceit? Would there be children? *Could* there be? Would her staff ever accept him as one of them? Wasn't there something else he had to tell her...?

Blackness darker than the sky of Gizelle's place took him at last.

Chapter 32

Scarlet could feel the tiny flicker of life in Mal's chest, the slow, tired sparkle of it, just as she could feel the soul-deep weariness that had driven his body to collapse. For a long moment, she only held him, while the warm rain slowed to nothing as the wyrm's power dissipated.

She had expected victory to feel... like victory.

But there was no sense of celebration to the scene.

The wyrm, frozen out of time, was stretched from the edge of her battered rain forest, across dozens of crushed cottages, to the cracked, tiled expanse of the pool deck. Columns lay scattered in coins of concrete, as if she had gone for Greek *ruins* in her architecture aesthetic.

She did not need to be an engineer to know that the central buildings were a complete loss. What wasn't caved in had been badly shaken, wind-damaged, and nearly washed away in the torrential rains. The pool had cracked; the water features were silent for the first time in years. The slopes were eroded, her trees—her precious, life-giving trees—had been toppled. The event hall appeared to have collapsed. Hedges had been stripped of flowers and leaves, leaving only bare sticks.

It was weirdly quiet, except for the sound of running water. All of the bugs and frogs and birds had been driven to ground by the rain and wind.

Scarlet closed her eyes, looking further. Mudslides showed dark scars through the green forest. Water still ran in rivulets all down the slopes of the island. Great swathes of jungle had been ripped up by the roots, washed away, or shredded in place.

Graham's garden and greenhouse had been flattened. The Den was still standing, but all of the windows had been shattered and half the roof ripped off; the interior was drenched and Bastian's hoard was scattered across the island. The other manors along the cliff were in similar shape. Half of the hotel had collapsed in on itself. Her office and her courtyard were sodden; the entire outside wall of her bedroom had fallen down, leaving the bones of the roof over an open room.

Tyrant...

She found him at once, safely—if not happily—huddled with Sweet One under the dumpster behind the kitchen, and relief flooded through her.

Tyrant was safe. They had evacuated in time. Everyone trapped here had survived. Her tree still stood. That was all that mattered.

But she couldn't quite keep tears from tracking down her face.

"Is he... *dead*?"

Scarlet looked up in alarm, to find Conall standing above them, Gizelle plastered against his side. The rest of the staff was picking through the rubble, clinging to their mates and assessing their wounds; no one was unscathed.

"No," she said swiftly, her arms tightening around Mal. "Only... tired."

She had never been so exhausted, either. Not even after Gizelle had tried to poison her.

"He... saved me," Conall said numbly. "But... *you* brought me back."

"Gizelle made it possible," Scarlet said wearily. "If your mate-bond had not kept you here a little while, I would not have been able to help you."

Slowly, painfully, Conall knelt beside her, hampered by Gizelle's iron grip on his side and his own obvious pain. "I am in your debt."

Scarlet laughed humorlessly. "That's probably good, because your share of the island doesn't have a lot of resale value right now. I'm afraid it has depreciated greatly over the last few hours."

Conall put his head down and for a moment Scarlet thought he was shaking in pain. Then he began to laugh, a halting, hesitant chuckle that bloomed into a great guffaw of humor.

Gizelle stared at him in alarm for a moment, then began to giggle helplessly.

Scarlet couldn't help herself, joining them in hysterical merriment, and soon everyone was in stages of shocky laughter, interspersed with tears and chatter.

"I'm fine," Amber assured Tony. "I promise, I'm *fine*."

"The baby..." Tony insisted. "We should get to the mainland and have you both checked. Does anyone have a working phone?"

No one did.

"I barely have working clothing," Breck pointed out, lifting the drenched shreds of his shirt.

"The baby is fine," Scarlet could tell Tony, at least. "A healthy, happy life spark." A sense of mischief overcame her. "And so is Laura's, and Lydia's."

"You knew?" Laura exclaimed over her mate's arm as Tex enfolded her in a protective hug.

Wrench was staring at his mate in surprise. "You... you're..."

Lydia's smile was slow and stunning. "I only knew I might be," she said, shaking her head. She gave Scarlet a sly, sideways look. "It was going to be a surprise!"

"He looks surprised to me," Travis pointed out.

Wrench was still standing with his arms limp at his side and his mouth open, unable to form complete sentences, or even, apparently, full words.

"What about me?" Breck joked irrepressibly. "Am *I* pregnant?"

Darla punched him in the arm and said, "Ouch! We have a bruise there." She twisted her arm to inspect her purpling flesh.

Scarlet gave a sigh, and felt it ripple through the island.

The clouds overhead were beginning to thin, with shafts of sunlight burning through. Mist clouded over the ground, and gradually the surviving insects started to sing. The breeze from the ocean was friendly again and Scarlet could feel her trees getting down to the business of growing again, slowly putting out new branches and sprouting new leaves to replace the ravaged canopy.

They were all *alive*.

Scarlet carried Mal to her room and salvaged enough of a bed to make him comfortable while he regained consciousness.

Chef insisted on feeding everyone, and somehow managed to make a hot meal from the ruins of his powerless kitchen;

Travis assembled a working grill from broken parts and Graham and Alice scavenged fruit and vegetables from destroyed greenhouse. Bastian bandaged up anyone who needed it, though no one was in worse shape than he was... except Mal.

They found enough tables and working chairs to put together a makeshift feast. The mood was light, and still a little stunned.

Tyrant and Sweet One, desperately offended by the day's events, made an appearance as Chef brought out dessert. Gizelle tried to cuddle with Sweet One, but the young cat had no interest in the gazelle shifter's comfort and yowled her way out of Gizelle's arms after only a few moments.

Tyrant, by contrast, wanted nothing more than to attach herself to Scarlet's ankles, constantly underfoot as Scarlet investigated the debris for anything that could be salvaged.

She was standing at the back of the restaurant deck holding a dented soup ladle when Gizelle found her.

"Be careful, Gizelle," Scarlet warned. "The deck isn't sound here."

Sweet One was being groomed vigorously by Tyrant on a broken table that was starting to dry in the baking sun.

Gizelle crept forward carefully to stand next to Scarlet.

"I didn't want to hurt you," she said mournfully.

"I know you didn't," Scarlet said. "I don't blame you."

"It was..."

"It wasn't your fault."

"But I..."

Scarlet turned to face her. "Good people blame themselves, Gizelle. Because good people take responsibility for what they do. I can only guess what it was like with that wyrm in your head, and you did the very best you could and I would never hold that against you."

"Am I a *good* person?" Gizelle asked plaintively.

"The very best," Scarlet assured her. "You are braver and better than anyone I know. And you are merciful, which is much, much harder than being merely good."

Gizelle stood still a moment and the loudest sounds were Sweet One's trilling protests as Tyrant held her down and licked her ears.

"It's quieter now," she observed. "In my head, I mean." She cocked her head at Scarlet curiously. "Does this mean I'll be normal?"

"I am not sure any of us are normal," Scarlet said dryly. "But that's not something you should aspire to anyway."

Gizelle gave her a swift, grateful hug. "I can hear your forest," she said, while her head was leaning against Scarlet's collarbone. "It sounds like *growing*."

Scarlet squeezed her back and let her go gather Sweet One into her arms. The kitten decided that Gizelle's attention was preferable to being further mauled by Tyrant and purred as she was picked up.

Scarlet collected Tyrant into her own arms and was given purring head-butts and vocal complaints. "Let's go see if your cat food survived," Scarlet suggested.

Chapter 33

Mal jerked awake at the attack, blindly reaching for his magic and finding that his stores were still empty.

It was just as well; the ferocious assailant was only Tyrant, who had decided that Mal's toes beneath the light quilt were clearly prey.

Mal sat up, precipitating a strategic retreat on the part of the kitten, and tried to figure out why Scarlet's room felt so odd.

He finally realized that it was missing an entire wall.

Where there had been tall windows and French doors, there was now... nothing. There was still a roof above, but the rest of the room was in ruins.

Ruins seemed an apt description for the entire resort, Mal decided. He hauled himself from the bed, which was only an air mattress on a sodden box spring; the original mattress, soaked, was standing on end in a pile of broken glass.

His muscles were reluctant to answer his demands, and he was glad to find a column that had survived the damage to lean against, looking out over the resort.

All that remained of the storm were tatters of dark clouds reflecting sunset colors across the darkening sky.

"It would be nice if we could take care of that before the civil guard got here," Scarlet said.

The doorway she stood in didn't hold a door any longer, and the jamb was splintered.

She, of course, looked perfectly put together in the midst of all the chaos: her hair swept back, her expression unruffled. Tyrant twined around her ankles, purring.

"Take care of what, now?" The sight of her drove every thought from his mind but one.

"The giant, frozen, feathered, two-headed beast that is crushing half of my resort. Most of the damage can be attributed to the storm and the earthquakes... but it's a little hard to explain that part."

"You know, you aren't supposed to disturb things until the insurance adjuster has had a chance to see the site," Mal said lightly. "You can get ugly lawsuits doing that."

"I'm pretty sure my insurance doesn't cover attack by angry ancient creatures, anyway," Scarlet said dryly. "And I'm vastly underinsured for this anyway."

"Insurance policies are put together by amateurs," Mal scoffed. He started to step towards her, and decided that holding onto the column was a better choice.

In a blink, Scarlet was at his side, her arm up under his. "It can wait," she said softly. "You should rest more."

As she led him back to the bed, giving him no choice in the matter, Mal had to ask, "Everyone? Everyone is okay?"

"Bruised and battered," Scarlet said gravely. "But no injuries that won't heal after a few shifts and some good meals."

"Your tree?" Mal asked reluctantly. Visions of the great rainforest trees being sucked into the raging storm had been firmly placed into his collection of nightmare fodder.

"A few fallen branches," Scarlet said calmly, helping him settle back into the bed. "But my leaves will grow back. I'll flower again."

"What happens now?" Mal asked, not releasing her.

Scarlet gazed at him. "I... don't know."

"Do you want to rebuild?"

Scarlet sighed and sat beside him. "I... I want to. But..."

"Money's no object," Mal reminded her.

Scarlet regarded him thoughtfully. "It doesn't feel right," she admitted.

"Would it feel better if it came through your staff?"

Scarlet smiled faintly. "It might. But they've already tapped everything they had just to buy this place." She looked wryly through the missing wall over the savaged resort. "For all the good it will do them. I bankrupted us all when I asked you to accept the offer."

"But you saved the world," Mal pointed out. "Oh, and they haven't begun to tap their resources." He had remembered the other thing he needed to tell Scarlet.

She looked at him suspiciously. "What are you on about now?"

Mal didn't have the energy to bait her further, though his dragon wearily admitted it might have been fun. "Darla's hoard. It's not locked."

Scarlet blinked at him and furrowed her brow. "What?"

Mal chuckled. "It's not locked. Those bracelets that were sent for Darla's engagement? Those were a gift commissioned by her father. That they were activated shows his blessing; she never needed her mother's. The hoard is hers. She has wealth that pales even mine, and she could give you enough to rebuild the entire island, pay off your debt, pave the road from the airstrip, put in an amusement park, and hire celebrity musicians every night without even noticing the difference."

Scarlet's face went from astonished, through amazed, to angry in the blink of an eye. "You're telling me that you've let Darla and Breck believe that they gave up the hoard to be together and this *whole time* they've had access to it?"

"Resources hold amazing bargaining power," Mal said apologetically. "I knew I'd lose that advantage over you if I told them because they would already give you the shirts from their backs if you asked."

Scarlet opened and closed her mouth several times, then sighed and laughed helplessly. "I suppose I understand that," she admitted, shaking her head. "It doesn't mean I entirely forgive it," she added threateningly. "They suffered so needlessly!"

Mal took her hand. "I shall endeavor to earn your absolution in the future," he promised. "And I will tell Darla and Breck myself and fall upon their mercy."

"I think that they are feeling fairly merciful," Scarlet said, amused. "Given that you've just saved the world and healed Conall."

"*We've* saved the world," Mal reminded her. "And *you* are the one who brought Conall back."

"We make a good team," Scarlet murmured, leaning her forehead against his.

Mal kissed her, and ran out of air long before he wanted to.

"I have a question for you," he said, when Scarlet released him.

"Ask," Scarlet said gently.

"Will you marry me, Scarlet Stanson? Will you be my partner as well as my mate? Will you allow me to bring my hoard here and give you half of it as my wife? You can fund your own rebuild, with your own money, and keep your pride as well as your resort."

Scarlet wiped her eyes. "Are you trying to offer me a buyout in order to get me to marry you?" she demanded.

"Dammit," Mal said with a laugh. "Old habits die hard."

She was smiling like the sun behind her tears and surely, somewhere, there were riots of rainbows from the combination.

"Yes," she said. "I will marry you. I will take half of your hoard and give you half of my island and all of my heart and the rest of my life. I love you, Mal Padrikanth Moore."

Mal gathered her into his aching arms and kissed her until the resort burst into bloom around them.

Epilogue

M al looked out over the building site and had to smile.

"It's amazing what magic portals and unlimited funds can do in a few years," Scarlet observed, suddenly at his side.

"Having the ability to instantly landscape doesn't hurt anything," Mal added.

The resort was already rebuilt to its former shining glory and it was hard to tell that any trees or gardens had ever been damaged. It was, if anything, more beautiful, more luxurious, and more alive. There were new pools, a grander event hall, and the hotel had been built to effortless modern standards. Chef's kitchen had gone from good to gleaming. Solar panels shimmered from every roof, marking the resort's near independence from fuel. A broad dish near the top of the island promised better connectivity... and *mostly* delivered it.

When the last of the big work on the resort had been completed and the finishing touches were nearly done, the construction efforts had moved up the island. The resort was on the south tip, facing west for the best sunsets. Along the cliffs that went north on the east coast, where the Den had stood, there were new luxury and family cottages for month-long getaways, complete with kitchens.

They were standing further north yet, tucked away from the resort, looking out onto a bustling construction site. The center of the little village was already complete; the elders' housing, the medical center, and the school had all been priorities for the new residents, and little houses were growing around them organically, some of them still covered in blue tarps as roof work was being completed.

"Come and see the new playground," Scarlet invited. There was an unexpected sparkle to her eyes, and a mischievous quirk to her mouth. Mal was instantly suspicious.

But Scarlet only took his hand, and strolled innocently with him down the road into the village.

They passed a small sports field, and a simple community pool, Graham's second greenhouse, and the lot where Neal was running an excavator to make space for the footings for a combination restaurant and movie theater.

A tiny general store was open for business and Mal nodded to the woman sweeping in front of it.

The playground was already being broken in. Several children in a wide range of ages were playing across the metal framework of a dragon with a slide for a tail and monkey bars across its chest cavity. Swings hung from the spread wings and an older boy was gently pushing three younger children in turn.

Mal hadn't even realized that there *were* that many children on the island yet, but the little community had been slowly expanding as the infrastructure was finished and the resort was already nearly up to full capacity.

"The school will be opening up this fall," Scarlet said, with a nod to the long, low building that flanked one edge of playground. "Travis' sister has experience running an isolated, rural

K-12 and I think the staff of teachers that she helped select will be a good fit here."

"I imagine this will at least be a nice change from the wilds of Alaska," Mal observed.

"It's certainly warmer," Scarlet chuckled.

One of the children on the monkey bars gave a sudden shriek and fell... only to shift midair into a black-winged panther and glide easily down onto the sand below amid the shreds of his clothing.

"Lydia's going to have words about the clothes. I think that's the third outfit this week," Scarlet said with a tolerant smile.

The children he'd been playing with scrambled down to help collect the pieces of his shirt and shorts.

"Your mom is going to be mad," a little dark-skinned girl said firmly, holding up the shorts, split along the seams.

The winged panther turned back into a little dark-haired boy. He took the shorts gravely, and attempted to put them back on. The older boy who had been pushing the swings supplied a series of safely pins from a pocket and helped him reassemble them into something that would keep him covered.

From around the corner of the community hall, there was a sudden clatter of hooves and a tiny gazelle came bolting out into the playground, pursued by a white-haired woman who was nearly as fleet on two bare feet as the foal was on four.

"You have to eat lunch before we play!" Gizelle chided, her voice full of laughter.

The little antelope darted through the metal columns of the playground dragon and drew up short against a broad, shovel-shaped pair of antlers as a giant stag suddenly appeared through the brush beyond.

The sharp stop proved too much for the gazelle in the loose sand and it tumbled over itself to bounce up as a toddler girl with a head full of dark curls. "Papa!" she burbled in glee. She grasped the antlers in two tiny hands and was lifted high into the air at the crown of the huge Irish elk that had blocked her path.

Gizelle came to a chortling stop at Conall's feet. "Clothes, Jana! We're supposed to be people right now. In clothes!"

"No clothes," Jana protested. "No clothes!"

But she let Gizelle scoop her up from Conall's rack and wrapped chubby arms around her neck.

"Miss Scarlet!" The dark-skinned girl had spotted Scarlet standing with Mal at the edge of the playground. "Miss Scarlet! Did you see the dragon? Mr. Neal made us a dragon!"

"I saw it, Amy!" Scarlet said warmly. "He made a wonderful dragon."

The other children gathered around them eagerly. "Will you do it, Miss Scarlet? Will you?"

"I wanna flower!" one of the youngest demanded.

Scarlet grinned and the hedge they were standing next to burst into bloom. She and Mal walked away to the sound of squeals and delight as the children began to gather them.

"It's almost finished," Mal observed. "Have you thought about what you want to do with Beehag's compound while we've still got all the construction equipment and workmen? Knock what's left to the ground? Build a monument?"

Scarlet's eyes crinkled into her smile. "I wanted to see what you thought about building a school there."

Mal's eyes flickered to the school in the center of the village but he immediately realized that she had something very different in mind. "What kind of school?" he asked.

"A boarding high school for shifters," Scarlet said, watching his face. "Perhaps with an emphasis on biology and pre-law; the arboretum is an amazing resource, and both you and Amber have mentioned being interested in teaching. Being a shifter in public school isn't always easy, and it would be nice if we could give kids a safe place to be themselves and learn with others who are like them while they are navigating all the problems of growing up."

An unexpected surge of interest swelled in Mal. He'd never considered teaching *seriously*, but now that it was on the table, he couldn't get the idea out of his head. "I know some professors," he said thoughtfully. "Would we do just secondary? Or post-secondary? I'd need to find some good education advisors, research the standards, find out what the legalities are in Costa Rica."

"Would you teach magic?"

Mal drew to a stop. "I... I don't know." Once, he'd thought he would have to, to train a new fighter to battle the wyrm hundreds of years in the future. But he didn't *need* to do that now.

"We'd probably have to level what's there now and build something completely new," Scarlet said, squeezing his arm. "There's a lot of time to think about it."

"It wouldn't have to be limited to shifters," Mal observed. "We could welcome other magical creatures, like mermaids... and dryads."

Scarlet's delighted smile grew smoky with secrets. "I have something to show you," she said mysteriously.

Mal stopped thinking about the school. "I love your sur-prises," he said honestly. The only secrets they kept from each other now were purely for the joy of it.

"Portal to my tree?" Scarlet invited, and she vanished play-fully.

Mal traced a doorway in the air and murmured the words as he gestured, then stepped through to Scarlet's familiar clear-ing.

Scarlet wasn't by her tree. Mal looked around curiously to find her at the far edge of the clearing, kneeling in the flowers.

He could feel her pride and eagerness through their mate-bond, shimmering bright with anticipation, and her smile as she lifted her head to watch him approach was nearly as bril-liant.

She stood at the last moment and took his hand.

Wordlessly, overflowing with excitement, she led him to where three saplings with feathery, fern-like leaves were grow-ing in a little clear space together. They were knee-high and swaying in the slight breezy.

Mal had to glance back at Scarlet's scarred tree. It had the same distinctive leaves as the little sprouts.

"Are these...?"

"I don't know if they will be dryads," Scarlet confessed. "But I have never had saplings before, and they feel... more aware than other trees. Different. I don't know!"

She was looking at him with what might have been anx-iousness in someone lesser and Mal realized that he was still staring in shock. He gave a great whoop of laughter and pulled Scarlet into his arms so he could twirl her around until he was dizzy and laughing. A soft bed of moss met them as he pulled her over, laughing and kissing and rolling with her.

When he could catch his breath, he took her hand and kissed the simple gold ring he'd put there. "This may be the best surprise yet," he said.

"I never knew you wanted children," Scarlet said, caressing his cheek with her other hand.

"I never did either," Mal confessed. "And to be honest, I wasn't sure how that would work. But it seems like a marvelous idea."

Scarlet pulled his mouth to hers. "I have other marvelous ideas," she said suggestively. "Did I ever warn you about that lusty nature of dryads?"

"What about the children?" Mal asked teasingly.

"They're still asleep..."

Implications of the future suddenly occurred to Mal and he sat up. "I am going to have three girls like *you*," he groaned. "If they have your lusty nature, I'm going to have to steal Graham's machete to scare off boys and beat back interested trees."

Scarlet laughed and sat up. "Or we could raise them to understand who they are, have sensible boundaries, and deal with their own boys. Maybe one of them will *be* a boy."

Mal paused. "*Are* there boy dryads?"

"I haven't the faintest idea," Scarlet confessed.

"What does all of this *mean*?" Mal felt pleased and proud and more than a little panicked.

"I haven't the faintest idea," Scarlet repeated, a slow smile blossoming on her face.

"I'm going to have to do some research," Mal said. "Start a college trust. Pick names!"

Scarlet wrapped her arms around his neck. "We have *time,*" she said sweetly, kissing his ear.

It was still a strange feeling, not having a destination for his life. Mal still hadn't gotten used to the idea that there was nothing looming in his future that *had* to be done, a destiny that he had to be ready for, a task of such weight and importance that it overshadowed anything else that he did.

He got to choose now, how to spend his time—and who to be with—without constantly thinking about how it impacted his final objective.

He put a wondering hand to Scarlet's face and she closed her eyes and leaned into it.

Mal knew what to do with *this* time and he pulled Scarlet close to kiss her deeply.

Across the island, trees burst into bloom.

What's Next?

It's bittersweet indeed to bring the Shifting Sands Resort tale to end. I am so grateful to all my readers for their enthusiasm and investment, and I am so happy that I was able to share this journey with all of you. I love these characters, and it's terribly hard to say goodbye.

I do plan to return to Shifting Sands, eventually. I've got some other big projects to work on first, but this Christmas, keep an eye out for a Christmas story of Magnolia and Chef, which will be free at my website! (If you aren't on my mailing list or a member of my VIP group on Facebook, consider signing up or joining to get updates: zoechant.com) I also plan to put out one or two collections of short stories in 2020 – Liam will be getting his happy ever after and I have a number of other tales I would like to write up, including Bastian's arrival at the resort, and Tex's first day. I have already written the (very sad) story of Gizelle's parents, and a few other short treats to include.

After that... I'm not sure. Explore the idea of the Shifting Sands school? Cozy mysteries being solved by Liam's elders in the new Shifting Sands Bay? Do you want to find out what happens to the children of the staff? Are there any short stories you'd like to read that I should be sure to include in the collections? You can email me any time at zoechante-books@gmail.com and let me know.

Don't forget to leave reviews if you enjoyed the series! I read every one, and they mean the world to me.

Thank you again for reading my books! Readers like you keep me writing!

~Zoe

PS: The covers of the Shifting Sands Resort series were designed by Ellen Million. Visit her webpage at ellenmillion.com for coloring pages of several of my characters, including Gizelle and Hugh from the Fire and Rescue series, and look for signed bookplates!

More Paranormal Romance by Zoe Chant

D*ancing Bearfoot.* (**Green Valley Shifters # 1**). A single dad from the city + his daughter's BBW teacher + a surprise snow storm = a steamy story that will melt your heart.

Bodyguard Bear. (**Protection, Inc. # 1**). A BBW witness to a murder + the sexy bear shifter bodyguard sworn to protect her with his life + firefights and fiery passion = one hot thrill ride!

Bearista. (**Bodyguard Shifters # 1**). A tough bear shifter bodyguard undercover in a coffee shop + a curvy barista with an adorable 5-year-old + a deadly shifter assassin = a scorching thrill ride of a romance!

Firefighter Dragon. (**Fire & Rescue Shifters # 1**). A curvy archaeologist with the find of a lifetime + a firefighter dragon shifter battling his instincts + a priceless artifact coveted by a ruthless rival = one blazing hot romance!

Royal Guard Lion (**Shifter Kingdom #1**). A curvy American shocked to learn that she's a lost princess + a warrior lion shifter sworn to protect her + a hidden shifter kingdom in desperate need of a leader = a sizzling romance fit for a queen!

Find many more at Zoe's Amazon page!

Zoe Chant on Audio

Dancing Bearfoot – Audiobook - A single dad from the city + his daughter's BBW teacher + a surprise snow storm = a steamy story that will melt your heart.

Kodiak Moment – Audiobook - A workaholic wildlife photographer + a loner bear shifter + Alaskan wilderness = one warming and sensual story.

Hero Bear - Audiobook - A wounded Marine who lost his bear + a BBW physical therapist with a secret + a small town full of gossips = a hot and healing romance!

Zoe Chant, writing under other names

Rails; A Novel of Torn World by Elva Birch. License Master Bai knows better than to dream about his Head of Files, Ressa. A gritty and glamorous steampunk-flavored novel of murder, sex, unrequited love, drugs, prostitution, blackmail, and betrayal.

Laura's Wolf (**Werewolf Marines # 1**), by Lia Silver. Werewolf Marine Roy Farrell, scarred in body and mind, thinks he has no future. Curvy con artist Laura Kaplan, running from danger and her own guilt, is desperate to escape her past. Together, they have all that they need to heal. A full-length novel.

Mated to the Meerkat, by Lia Silver. Jasmine Jones, a curvy tabloid reporter, meets her match in notorious paparazzi and secret meerkat Chance Marcotte. A romantic comedy novelette.

Handcuffed to the Bear (Shifter Agents # 1), by Lauren Esker. A bear-shifter ex-mercenary and a curvy lynx shifter searching for her best friend's killer are handcuffed together and hunted in the wilderness. Can they learn to rely on each other before their pasts, and their pursuers, catch up with them? A full-length novel.

Keeping Her Pride (Ladies of the Pack # 1), by Lauren Esker. Down-and-out lioness shifter Debi Fallon never meant to fall in love with a human. Sexy architect and single dad Fletcher Briggs has his hands full with his adorable 4-year-old... who turns into a tiny, deadly snake. Can two ambitious people overcome their pride and prejudice enough to realize the only thing missing from their lives is each other?

Wolf in Sheep's Clothing, by Lauren Esker. Curvy farm girl Julie Capshaw was warned away from the wolf shifters next door, but Damon Wolfe is the motorcycle-riding, smoking hot alpha of her dreams. Can the big bad wolf and his sheep shifter find their own happy ending? A full-length novel.

Made in the USA
Coppell, TX
26 October 2019